A BROKEN SUN

Aditya Iyengar writes novels, screenplays, poetry and advertising copy. His previous books include *The Thirteenth Day* and *Palace of Assassins*. He enjoys writing mythological and historical fiction, and epic fantasy novels. He spends his time between Delhi and Mumbai.

A BROKEN SUN

ADITYA IYENGAR

Published by
Rupa Publications India Pvt. Ltd 2018
7/16, Ansari Road, Daryaganj
New Delhi 110002

Sales Centres:

Allahabad Bengaluru Chennai
Hyderabad Jaipur Kathmandu
Kolkata Mumbai

Copyright © Aditya Iyengar 2018

All rights reserved.
No part of this publication may be reproduced, transmitted,
or stored in a retrieval system, in any form or by any means,
electronic, mechanical, photocopying, recording or otherwise,
without the prior permission of the publisher.

This is a work of fiction. Names, characters, places and incidents are
either the product of the author's imagination or are used fictitiously and
any resemblance to any actual person, living or dead,
events or locales is entirely coincidental.

ISBN: 978-81-291-5131-5

First impression 2018

10 9 8 7 6 5 4 3 2 1

The moral right of the author has been asserted.

Printed by Thomson Press India Ltd., Faridabad

This book is sold subject to the condition that it shall not,
by way of trade or otherwise, be lent, resold, hired out, or otherwise
circulated, without the publisher's prior consent, in any form of binding or
cover other than that in which it is published.

Contents

Introduction / vii

The Thirteenth Night / 1

The Fourteenth Day / 7

The Fourteenth Night / 129

The Fifteenth Day / 135

The Fifteenth Night / 183

Epilogue / 198

Glossary / 200

INTRODUCTION

A Broken Sun is a sequel to *The Thirteenth Day* and follows from where the first novel ended—the death of Abhimanyu on the thirteenth day of the Kurukshetra war. As I've mentioned in the first novel, the books are set around 1000 BC during the Iron Age in India. My story hinges on the assumption that a small, dynastic war possibly took place around that period and was repeatedly embellished in its retelling to become the story we hear today.

I had an ulterior motive in setting the books around this age since it gave me an opportunity to pare out the 'myth' part of the story and leave out the supernatural weapons or happenings that influenced the war. I felt that they distracted the reader from the epic's true beauty—the characters that inhabit its text. My attempt has been to tell the story of these people as human beings with human problems, and not seemingly invincible demigods blessed with awe-inspiring powers.

A novel is bigger than its writer and the list of people who have contributed to this could fill up many pages. But we have a story to begin, so I will keep it short. A big thank you to Kapish Mehra and Rupa Publications for taking on this sequel,

Aparna Kumar who edited it with speed and unwavering clarity, Onkar Fondekar and Mugdha Sadhwani who designed the beautiful cover that caught your eye and brought you to this page.

As always, thank you Ma and Ashvin for all your love and support, and for bearing with my surly, curmudgeonly writer avatar.

THE THIRTEENTH NIGHT

ARJUNA

I REMEMBER, ABHIMANYU, that at the beginning of the war—the very beginning—I had second thoughts about the entire affair. There I was, in my chariot, holding my bow—the lucky one I call *Gandiva*—looking out at the vast rows of metal that hid so many favourite relatives from my childhood and youth. I could make out Guru Drona, Grandsire Bhishma, Uncle Salya and Bhagadatta, among many others. They had all loved me at some point of time, and perhaps still did.

Over the past few years, the mind had been trained to see them as enemies. 'Them' is perhaps a broad term. More specifically, Guru Drona and Grandsire Bhishma. I had readied myself for battle by reminding myself of 'them', day and night. I had even repeated their names to myself during the thirteen years of exile like a mantra whenever I had to work up some anger.

That morning, however, it was my body that let me down. My knees buckled, the armour felt heavy, the helmet seemed to clamp onto my skull, threatening to crush it. My arm began shaking and *Gandiva* nearly slipped from my grasp. Your Uncle Krishna noticed this and asked me what the matter was.

You see, as a veteran of many wars himself, he knew that warriors like me did not shake before a fight unless it was something out of the ordinary. Nerves are not an affliction I'm cursed with.

I told him very honestly that I didn't know. I hadn't shivered before a fight for many years now. Maybe the idea of fighting and killing Grandsire and my Guru, along with my blood relatives was evoking a reaction from my body? Perhaps, despite my efforts at retraining my mind to hate them, there was still some part of me that loved them?

I could see their army in front of me. My mind knew that the next action was to draw the bow, nock an arrow and let it loose in their direction, but the body seemed to rebel against the thought. Looking back now, I'm almost ashamed of the way my body refused to do what my mind asked of it.

Death occupies a significant part of a Kshatriya's life. It is our craft. Potters make pots, poets recite verses, cowherds herd cows, and Kshatriyas, well, we kill.

And now, I had to kill the teachers who had taught me to kill.

They say the greatest reward for a teacher is when the student successfully applies his teachings on him, thus teaching the teacher that even his knowledge is finite.

But there would be scant reward in this for them or me. I asked Krishna whether all this made sense. Did this war really need to happen? Yes, there was a lot in it for us. A kingdom for one, and the opportunity to decide who would rule it—once and forever. But would the kingdom even be worth it without Grandsire or Guru Drona?

Your uncle sighed and replied patiently to his credit. If I had told your Uncle Bhima I was having second thoughts about fighting moments before the war, he would have probably begun the carnage by assaulting me.

What Krishna told me that day changed the way I looked at the war, and that's why, after much delay, I'm imparting it to you in a crude manner, without the finesse of your uncle. Maybe one day after all this is over, I'll tell you exactly what he said in more detail. But for now, this is enough; it is important to do the task at hand and not worry about the consequences. Your actions are in your control, but the rest is not. Focus on what is happening at the moment. Don't pre-empt a positive or negative result. A warrior's duty is to do the best they can in a war, regardless of who they are facing.

Does this make sense? I hope so. Nothing seems to make much sense these days.

I've never really spoken to you, my son. Conversation is a terrible tool for expression. I preferred to present myself as an example instead, and hoped you would observe and learn from it. This may have been a mistake. Sometimes, I suppose, it is best to use crude or imperfect tools, rather than none at all. But we all must learn from our mistakes. The task at hand for me is to talk to you now.

You are listening to me, aren't you?

THE FOURTEENTH DAY

RADHEYA

Sanjaya Gavalgani was an odd bird.

He looked like one to begin with. A large, hooked, beak-like nose, small beady eyes, and a head that was round and bald at the top but surrounded by a thin forest of hair. The skin seemed to hang off his thin arms and spindly legs, but a small paunch drooped proudly and defiantly in front of his dhoti. The soldiers called him 'The Owl' for it was believed that Sanjaya never slept. He saw everything with those small eyes of his, and heard everything through those large ears that had thickets of hair sprouting from them which he would stroke every now and then when in deep thought.

He wore a torn shawl paired with a shabby dhoti that was stained at the back—by what I could only hope was mud—in the sabha that morning. He held the Speaking Staff loosely in a hollow ring between his thumb and forefinger.

'Fifty-two thousand, one hundred and thirty-five men dead, only yesterday. Seventy-six incapacitated. Eighteen hundred and nine equines, including horses, mares, and donkeys, dead or incapacitated.'

'Did you include yourself in the incapacitated donkeys' list?'

spoke a voice from the back.

The sabha tent rumbled with laughter, though without the enthusiasm of a couple of days back. There were less Kaurava allies now. As Sanjaya's numbers seemed to suggest, yesterday—the thirteenth day—had been particularly brutal. Grandsire Bhishma had little use of him, as did Drona, and even though he recited his numbers every morning in the sabha, no one paid much attention to him until today, when he announced that more than half the army was dead.

Yesterday's losses had simply been too great, with only a minor victory in the form of Abhimanyu's death. The five Pandavas still remained on the field, as did Dhristadyumna, his father Drupada, and Virata.

'May I continue?' Sanjaya asked formally. Suyodhana glowered at him, but Drona nodded.

'Three thousand, one hundred and thirty-nine elephants dead or incapacitated.'

'Are you going to include all these details in your next dispatch?' Suyodhana interrupted.

'Yes,' Sanjaya replied, in a matter-of-fact manner.

Suyodhana shook his head even as there was a minor uproar in the sabha. Sanjaya Gavalgani was Dhritarashtra's treasurer and adviser. Over the years, he had also acquired his trust. Not a small thing, given that Dhritarashtra was quite miserly with it. Sanjaya was, Dhritarashtra proclaimed, the only man who could provide him with an opinion untainted by emotion, and I believed him. Love, hate or any emotion, for that matter, seemed alien to Sanjaya. One could not tell if he was happy, sad or indifferent, or if he had ever felt these emotions at all, and whether he would even recognize them if he felt them. Sanjaya had no friends and no family, save the royal one—at least to the best of my knowledge.

He had acquired a reputation throughout the kingdom for his loyalty to the blind king and his skills in miserliness. A common joke doing the rounds was that even the mice that inhabited the royal coffers could only leave the premises with Sanjaya's signed approval. The junior treasurers called him 'Yamraja', after the God of death, since nothing ever left his fiefdom—the treasury—for the world of the living.

Courtesy was his armour, numbers were his weapon. Dhritrashtra had sent him along with Suyodhana, on the face of it, to provide the benefit of his experience. But it was actually to receive regular accounts of what was happening on the battlefield, knowing the ability of the bards to exaggerate.

There are some stories accountants tell better than bards.

At the end of each day, Sanjaya would tally all the losses—men, equipment and camp material—sourced through his innumerable associates who infested the camp like insects. He would then collate all the information in a single document that described the events of the day to its minutest detail, from the death of a king to the loss of a horse stirrup. The document would be given to a rider who answered only to the emperor much to Suyodhana's annoyance, and he blamed Sanjaya for providing a negative view of the war thus far.

'Tell me, Sanjaya,' said Suyodhana, snatching the Staff from him, 'do you enjoy reporting the numbers of our dead every day to my father?'

Sanjaya did not reply. Suyodhana continued, 'The Pandava forces are thinning drastically. I don't think I saw more than a brigade of elephants yesterday. Did you report this to my father? Speak!'

He tossed the Staff back to Sanjay who replied in a calm and measured tone, 'I report what I can verify.'

'How can you verify any of this unless you're on the battlefield?'

There were sniggers from the corners of the sabha tent. Sanjaya was no warrior. I doubt he had ever set foot in an *akhara* in his youth, or if he even had the experience of youth. He seemed perpetually aged—like he had come out of his mother's womb as a middle-aged man and had never looked back.

Sanjaya considered Suyodhana's suggestion for a moment and replied, 'I tally the day's figures and send them back. The dead, the wounded, the kings left among our allies. Just as your father asked me to.' He emphasized the word 'father'.

Suyodhana glowered again but did not say anything. Sanjaya was here as Dhritarashtra's man. To cross him would be to cross his father. Even Suyodhana knew that if anything happened to Sanjaya, the allies would lose their trust and think of him as someone headstrong enough to disobey his father. We couldn't afford to lose any allies.

Drona took the Speaking Staff and began, 'Leave Sanjaya out of this. He has his job, as do we. Now, yesterday was a victory. Let's not diminish it. We killed more soldiers than we lost and this was partly because the Samsaptakas held off the Indraprastha contingent while the *chakravyuha* ground out the rest of their army.' The kings in the sabha hooted and cheered.

'Some of you had a word with me this morning and I agree that this war has gone on for long enough. But the war will not be over until we capture or kill Yudhishthira. So, we have to conserve our troops while killing theirs until our numbers can come to bear.'

The old fox didn't look well. His eyes were red and his face was criss-crossed by worry lines. The blackness of his hair had been overpowered by grey and his voice, that had once frightened the birds from the trees, had been beaten into a thin, hoarse whisper.

'So today, we'll go for something more defensive than the *chakravyuha*, but equally capable of throttling the Pandavas if need be. The van will be in the form of a box formation, a *sakata*, and behind that, we will have the reserve arranged in a *chakravyuha*, just in case we have to change tactics and go on the offensive. I will be in the van of the *sakata* along with Suyodhana, Sushasana and Shakuni. The reserve contingent will be manned by the fighters who were in the thick of the action yesterday—Radheya, Jayadratha, Bhurisravas, Ashwatthama, Vrishasena, and Kripa. Jayadratha shall be at the centre of the formation and exposed to the fighting only when there is no other option. He really stretched himself yesterday, so we should let him rest until there is absolutely no alternative.'

He beamed at Jayadratha and the kings nodded in agreement. Jayadratha had been magnificent yesterday. Not a single Pandava had been able to pierce our formation after Abhimanyu broke into the *chakravyuha*. And it was solely because of Jayadratha.

I was more concerned about Drona. He was putting himself in front for the fourth day in a row. Ever since Grandsire Bhishma had fallen, he had taken it upon himself to win the war. I did not have the authority to overrule the judgement of the supreme general of our army but I was senior enough to question it without being dismissed altogether. I raised my arm and the

Speaking Staff was delivered to me.

'My Lord Drona, you may need some rest yourself. Let me take your position in the van.'

Drona shook his head before I could even finish my sentence.

'No, I will get Yudhishthira today.'

'It's hardly necessary to get him. Now that Abhimanyu is dead, I don't think peace is on the cards.'

Yuyutsu, Suyodhana's brother, snorted from the back but was ignored by the sabha. He supported the Pandava cause while still fighting for his brother. To what end I didn't fully understand. He probably disliked Suyodhana since he himself was too far down the hierarchy of heirs to be king. Maybe he felt he could draw a favourable outcome whichever side won. It probably says a lot about Suyodhana that he did not throw him in prison for treason. I probably would have.

We were a crew of many colours, mostly kingdoms that had something to gain by way of territory or iron. Many kings secretly supported the Pandava cause too but found it more convenient to join ours. Abhimanyu's death had bothered all of them, not just because of its sheer brutality, but also due to the fact that an untested boy could penetrate our ranks with such disdain.

Where last night there was celebration, the morning brought along cold reflection. The question that was running through everyone's mind was the same. Did the Pandavas hold more surprises like young Abhimanyu? And if Sanjaya was correct, and yesterday had in fact been a day of great losses, how much more could we lose?

I had no answer to this. I had already lost more than they ever could—a family and a kingdom. But now was not the time for self-pity. When the time would come to dictate my life story, it would all come out, and a bard would tell my story. A proper one, who would sing it with some skill and perhaps lift it out of the stables. Not a word till then.

'Let me lead the line with you, sire. I'm good with elephants.'

All the eyes in the sabha followed the voice till it led to Surmashana, Sushasana's son, who had dealt the mortal blow to Abhimanyu yesterday. He had been given the privilege of attending the council today by Suyodhana for doing the needful on Abhimanyu when no one else was willing to.

'I killed Abhimanyu yesterday,' he said confidently, reminding the sabha of his credentials.

'Killing a weakened warrior is no show of strength. Do not think for a moment that today will be easy. Arjuna and Bhima do not make foolhardy runs into the centre of an enemy formation. They will rip us apart from the outside,' snapped Drona.

Surmashana looked like he wanted to melt into the earth and never be seen again.

'It might not be a bad idea, come to think of it,' said Shakuni, the king of Gandhara and uncle to Suyodhana. I could almost hear his mind whirring as he spoke.

'Imagine this,' he said, framing an invisible picture with his hands, 'the slayer of the great warrior Abhimanyu goes out to do battle with the Pandavas. The Kaurava's own boy-hero.' He shook the Staff and raised his voice as he spoke. 'It is important for our troops to know that we have diamonds that can shine given the right amount of heat. That a hero can come up from within them too!'

All of this was not strictly true, of course. The warrior class would never allow a common soldier to lead the line, not even if he was ten times the fighter Arjuna was.

He looked at me now. 'The Kaurava army has always loved its own. And it recognizes its heroes no matter how young, or no matter where they were born. This is true for Radheya, it is true for the boy-hero Surmashana too. The best get the best opportunities. That is the message we will give our forces today.'

There was little joy in the sabha at this announcement. Equal opportunity for all was not something most kings thought of or even cared about. Some of the allies in the sabha cheered awkwardly but for the most part there was sullen silence. Drona shook his head but was clearly in no mood to argue. He looked at me as if asking for support; I shrugged my shoulders.

Suyodhana ended the discussion. 'Very well then, boy, you have your turn. You can lead the line with the elephants. But stay close to Drona and your father in the front. Do not stray away from them.' Surmashana bowed low in response and beamed at his father as he rose.

Drona finished the sabha with instructions on how the army would form that day. When he had finished, he walked out briskly with his head bowed low, refusing to make eye contact with anyone. I followed him outside.

'Drona,' I called out as he exited the tent. He looked at me and blinked, coming out of his own reverie.

'Formation's good. Will throw them off. I think they'll be expecting another *chakravyuha* today,' I said, trying to sound cheerful.

'War has changed. It used to be simpler. Or maybe it's just an old soldier's nostalgia,' he replied distractedly.

This was new. Drona, Iron Drona, talking about sentimental

slosh. What had gotten into him?

'War is still the same. Hacking, maiming, piercing, crushing. All the elements are still there, old man. Don't go soft on me,' I said, hoping to rile him. He smiled sadly at me. This was indeed strange. He had seemed fine last night.

'What has happened?' I asked.

He shook his head and ended the conversation by looking away and walking briskly towards his tent. I saw Suyodhana nearby and asked him about Drona's condition.

'Our allies surrounded him this morning. A lot of them can't continue this war for more than a day. The losses have been too great, they all have to get home, and the stench in our camp is well...'

Thirteen days of war and now the fourteenth, with no end in sight. I had heard murmurs of discontent from some of our allies, especially the ones from the far south and east who would have to make a great trek back after the whole business was done. Our *yavana* and mleccha mercenaries from across the seas too had begun to grumble. Winter would set in soon and they had to return to their little caves or wherever they dwelled. As for the stench, I found myself sympathizing with them. The wind carried the putrefying odour of the dead from the battlefield into our camp. We had all lit camphor and incense in the initial days to ward off the stench, but even that had become ineffective over the past two days. Most of us had learned to deal with it. But for how long?

'What did the allies say?'

'Well, they were angry and Guruji said they raised their voices more than once. Had I been there, I would have sent them packing.'

I could feel the pain in Suyodhana's voice. For all his talk, he needed them, and so did Drona. From being a leader of an alliance, he had been reduced to its dependent.

'Anyway, Ashwatthama came in and did my bit.'

I cringed inwardly. If there was anyone with less tact in the camp than Suyodhana or Sushasana, it was the imbecile son of Drona. A surly lout who kept to himself and spent his time sharpening arrows and giving them names.

'So how many of them will still fight?'

'Most, I guess. One of the advantages of having Sanjaya around is that with numbers, he is even better than a quartermaster. Two, maybe three thousand troops will leave our camp today after we move for the battlefield. I spoke to all the kings though. Hopefully, there will be a change of heart. I've also doubled the bounty on the heads of all the Pandavas. Hopefully, that will get the blood flowing through their arms again.'

Placing a bounty on kings and doubling it was nothing new. Especially since most kings led their troops personally. To kill them would send their entire faction into disarray, and that would make the slaughter easy. I had placed Narasimha as my de facto commander for the Anga contingent in case something happened to me. A lot of kings did not pre-empt such a condition as they believed themselves to be invincible. This idea that the lives of kings were the most crucial on a battlefield was taken up by the bards too. I don't think any of the regular soldiers found mention in the texts. At least not in the ones I knew of.

Poets tend to skip details. Accountants don't. I wondered what Sanjaya would make of the new bounty. He would probably provide an exact figure of debt owed and then the number of years it would take to repay it on the basis of current taxation laws, assuming of course, there was no drought.

But money could be sorted later. Warriors were the need of the hour. And a leader.

'Why is Drona still upset?' I enquired.

'Guruji,' he said with deliberate emphasis, 'is just feeling the strain of the past four days, I guess. I don't think the death of Abhimanyu went down well with him, although he's trying his best to not show it.'

'There are still five Pandavas to kill, including his favourite, Arjuna. How do you think he's going to feel then?' I asked.

'I don't know. He still thinks capturing Yudhishthira will end the war. I'm letting him have his way. He seems convinced.'

'I'm not sure it will, but…,' I shrugged and let the sentence drift into silence. There really was no telling what the outcome would be. Shatrujeet and Varahamira, my spies, had told me through their coterie of informants that the Pandavas considered me a major culprit in the act, along with Drona. A lot of the talk in their camp last night had been about retribution. Alternately, I was also hearing whispers about a certain lack of confidence in Pandava strategy.

They began the war with lesser troops than ours and were losing them at an equal pace. Abhimanyu's death brought these feelings to the fore. If they indeed had such great *atirathis* and *maharathis*, why did they place a boy at the head of their forces to get killed? The confidence they had placed in their commanders was ebbing. Could Arjuna, Bhima and Dhristadyumna really win the battle as they had claimed? And why did Yudhishthira stay determinedly at the back and allow his troops to get pulverized?

The war was tilting in our favour. If Drona managed to capture Yudhishthira from under their noses, who knew, maybe their soldiers and allies would lose confidence altogether? The thought was an interesting one, but I had no time to dwell on it. I walked back to my tent and found my retainer holding my armour. Narasimha was standing next to him. His glass eye gleamed in the sunlight.

'Reserves today, I hear,' he said, getting to the point.

I nodded as I removed my shawl and put on a light muslin tunic. My retainer mounted the rear piece of the plate armour on my back, then placed the front piece on my chest, and began fastening their leather straps together.

Narasimha watched this process and filled me in about my Anga contingent. We had only been on the field for three days now and hadn't taken so much a sustained whacking as much a sharp cuff to the ear. The losses hadn't been great, morale was still high.

'You need something,' Narasimha observed as my retainer worked busily on me.

'What's missing?' I muttered, checking the tightness of the strap.

'Arjuna has *Gandiva*. You need something too. A symbol. Something that tells the troops you're special.'

'I had two of those, remember? The earrings and the gold armour? And I gave them away too. There are enough expectations as it is. No point adding to them. Besides, you and I both know there is nothing special about *Gandiva*. And when I'm done with Arjuna, there will be nothing special about him either.'

'Troops are like children. Always happy when they have the

shiniest bauble in their hands. You need to give them something shiny.'

I rolled my eyes and changed the subject. 'Where is our position?'

'We're with Ashwatthama, Kripa, Bhurisravas—the prince of Bahlika—and Vrishasena, along with the Samsaptakas who are ahead of us and Jayadratha—the king of the Sindhus—who is behind us. Drona is riding with the elephants that will open up the Pandava formation and create a path for him. Samsaptakas will follow his troops.'

I smiled to myself. The Samsaptakas would not be happy. They were intense, bloodthirsty creatures. Many years ago, Arjuna's troops had destroyed the Trigarta kingdom and the Trigartas had been more than happy to ally with our cause just to kill him.

Three days back, led by their King Susharma, they had taken an oath to kill Arjuna and not leave the battlefield till he was dead, or they were. To this end, they gave up all their material possessions except for their armour and weapons, and even performed their death ceremonies and shaved off their hair. They wore white armour and fought with a hatred that I could only envy.

And I thought I had problems with Arjuna.

YUDHISHTHIRA

I AWOKE LATE at night in cold sweat and hastily wrapped a dhoti and shawl around myself, stepped over my slumbering retainer Vishakha, and walked towards Abhimanyu's tent. Had anyone bothered to empty it and hold his possessions till they could be sent to his wife Uttaraa?

Arjuna had been too distraught to even think about such details. All of us had been. I only hoped the scavengers had not come before me. I could hear a rustling sound from the tent as I approached it, and clenched my fist, ready to give a hiding to the first scavenger I saw.

The tent flap was open and I walked in quietly, resolved to catch the miscreant in the act. A figure was hunched over at the corner of the tent. With the exception of the figure and a solitary lamp that hung from a wooden beam at the top, the tent was empty. The figure turned.

It was Shikhandi. She turned around and saw me in the dim light of the tent. She guessed why I was there.

'I took the liberty of clearing out his tent. His belongings will be sent back to Uttaraa. I think that's what he would have wanted.'

'Yes, I think so,' I murmured, a little relieved at not having to brawl with a thief. She stood up and walked closer to the light. I saw her for the first time that evening. She wore a dhoti, a white cotton vest and shawl.

'My retainers have just finished emptying his tent. Don't worry, everything is safe.'

I looked around. It was surreal. Just a few hours ago, no one would have dared enter this tent out of fear of the occupant, much less forcibly haul out its possessions. And now it was empty, just like so many tents that speckled our side of the field.

'His armour is still on his body. Arjuna wanted to keep the body tonight before sending it back to Dwaraka tomorrow, while we fight. The body is in the tent near Arjuna's.' Shikhandi paused for a moment, before she continued, 'Arjuna was speaking to the corpse when I left him.'

I nodded dumbly. I had been rendered unconscious in the last hour of the battle yesterday. Shikhandi had recovered the body after the day's fighting. The next question stumbled out of my mouth.

'How bad was it?'

I couldn't see her face properly, but she was silent for a long time before answering.

'Do you really want to know?'

'Yes.'

The least I could do was show the boy the dignity of learning what his last moments were like, or trying to imagine it at least. For some strange reason, this made perfect sense to me. Was I going mad?

Shikhandi sighed and spoke. 'The armour protected him well. It was pierced and dented at a few places, but there was no real damage to his upper body. A few arrows were stuck on his legs but the wounds were not deep.'

She took a deep breath and continued, 'He was killed by a blow to the head. A mace, by the looks of it. The middle finger and third finger of his right hand were also severed. I think they first broke his chariot and weapons and then killed him. There are reports that he was fighting them off with a chariot wheel but I don't believe it. The fatal blow from the mace came from the back. He didn't see it coming, which is a small mercy, I suppose.'

She paused again and continued, 'I've heard it took six warriors to bring him down, Drona and Radheya included. And that was after his entire fighting force was killed. He was among the last to die.'

I closed my eyes and nodded, not knowing what to say, cursing myself for bringing the subject up. I think Shikhandi sensed as much as she walked passed me, out of the tent.

'Get some sleep, Yudhishthira. We have a long day ahead.'

I lumbered back to my tent and resisted the temptation to take something in order to sleep. I had failed Abhimanyu, as his uncle and as his senior commander on the battlefield. I did not know how Arjuna would take it. Would he look at me differently now? I was still his elder brother. Surely, he would remember that.

Tired thoughts. My mind had lost its ability to comprehend relationships anymore. I was always worried about losing one of my remaining family members or friends, either emotionally, or more likely, given we were in a war, physically. My brothers and I had drifted from each other during the war. We all chose to deal with our decision to fight and kill the people we had loved for so many years differently. I had thought most of these bonds had been broken the day the Kuru elders had sent us off on exile. But there was still a pang of sadness that crept in between the fear whenever Guruji came chasing after me.

I would not call him Guruji anymore. He did not deserve my respect or my fear. Perhaps calling him by his name shorn of any title would reduce the awe I felt for him. My brothers had done so a long time ago. I had persisted with calling him my Guru to remind myself that he was only doing his duty to the Kuru kingdom, and his mark on me was indelible and permanent. Perhaps by calling him Guruji, I had weakened my own arms that were trained not to strike an elder or a person of veneration.

The thoughts rolled over themselves till they became a confused mess. I was too tired to pick them apart rationally, so I gave up. This was not a battle I needed to win.

I tossed and turned till the light came in unannounced into my tent. Vishakha entered on cue with some neem twigs that I used to clean my teeth and hot towels. I finished my ablutions, put on a clean dhoti and tunic, and walked to the council tent.

The camp was bustling with activity in the morning, though with less vigour than a few days back. The killing had become mechanical over the past few days. No war any of us had participated in had lasted for more than a day or two. This war was already twelve days too long. No one had fought in a war with so many people before either. Most battles would involve a few thousand men. Here we were talking about hundreds of thousands from all over the world. If there was tactical naivety, it had to be forgiven on the grounds that no one had ever commanded armies of this size before. Factors like stench, camp scavenging or inflated prices of cremation ritual materials were simply not accounted for. Our costs had risen astronomically over the first few days. We would spend the rest of our lifetimes, and those of our children, repaying our allies and soldiers. Victory or defeat, this war had already dragged us into ruin. And yet, we needed to fight so that the ruins belonged to us.

Everyone had gathered. Bhima, Nakula and Sahadeva were talking among themselves. Drupada and Virata sat facing away from each other, young Chekitana sat next to Shikhandi who was explaining something to him, Dhristadyumna was looking intently at a chart of animal hide, and Arjuna sat in a corner with Krishna.

Our war council comprised kings who had donated the most men and resources to our cause. There weren't too many of them as almost everyone in Bharatvarsha had placed their bets on the Kauravas. Our council consisted of Drupada, the king of Panchala, and, as our father-in-law, the biggest donor to our cause. His son, Dhristadyumna and daughter Shikhandi were also in the council. Both were fine warriors and no one could grudge them their place. There was Virata of the Matsya kingdom, who had not taken kindly to a previous Kuru attempt to invade his land and had joined us principally to be the architect of Grandsire Bhishma's and Drona's downfall. With Bhishma incapacitated, half his battle, in a sense, was over. There was the young Prince Chekitana from the Chedi kingdom whose father had donated a few *ankinis* of men just so that his young son could see what war was like. A wise move. I doubted whether Chekitana would ever start a war in his life after seeing this. There were the Yadavas represented by our cousin Krishna and their General Satyaki. And there were the five of us, Pandavas.

The Kaurava council was a lot bigger than ours since they had more allies. My respect for Grandsire Bhishma had increased hugely for being able to steer all forty-odd of them. We had a hard enough time bringing consensus amongst twelve.

'Let's...er..begin,' said Dhristadyumna sombrely.

'Before we start, as the eldest member of our council, I would like to say something,' interrupted Virata.

He stood up slowly from his couch, cleared his throat loudly and began, 'I'm sorry for the loss of Abhimanyu. My condolences are with you, Arjuna, and all of you.'

He was visibly shaken though he was trying not to let it show. I noticed his hand tremble as he placed it on the couch and guided himself back to his seat. Abhimanyu had been his son-in-law, the husband of his widowed daughter Uttaraa. He needed condolences as much as Arjuna or any of us did. I was about to say something to this effect when Dhristadyumna began to speak.

'For today's...er...strategy, we need to consider several points. Firstly, our informer tells us that Drona is the commander-in-chief, but yesterday's formation was...uh...not something he could have devised. I conclude that Radheya was somehow involved in the strategy. Now, we don't have much information about the kinds of formations he prefers, or rather, let me take full responsibility, no one actually thought that he would ever be considered for a tactical role given how...uh... dependent the Kauravas are on Bhishma and Drona. Radheya's relationship with both of them has been fraught to say the least. We had studied the tactics of Bhagadatta and Salya, but we didn't anticipate that anyone else would provide a challenge tactically on the field.'

Smooth. No mention of the fact that we had not managed to penetrate the *chakravyuha* at all yesterday. None of us—*atirathis*, *maharathis*, and other men with countless years on the battlefield—had been able to get past the king of Sindhu, Jayadratha—a man of middling martial talent. The only one who did manage was a strip of a lad who had just had his first taste of war.

So we didn't have a plan, and here was Dhristadyumna, admitting shamelessly that we were powerless to stop Radheya's tactical ingenuity. But was he such a brilliant strategist after all? Or were we still reeling from yesterday's brutality? I decided not to speak up lest I was shot down and my lack of tactical awareness was exposed.

'Nonsense, it was just a one-off. Radheya doesn't have the brains for any tactical masterpiece. *Suta* is good with the bow but little else, and who wouldn't be if Parshurama trained them? Yesterday was a bad day, that's all,' said Bhima with finality.

Dhristadyumna smiled as I looked on dumbly, 'I hope… er…hope you…er…are right, Bhima.'

Drupada joined the chorus, 'Yes, he is, my boy. Radheya probably picked it up somewhere. I know his type. One trick, and then nothing. You watch. Today, we'll give him a hiding. You've been taught by the greatest war scholars in Bharatvarsha. There is no comparison. Bhima has said the most intelligent thing in the council today. One day up front does not make Radheya, Skanda, the God of war.'

I cringed inwardly, not at the reference to the celestial generalissimo—undefeated in all the stories we had heard as children—but at the fact that Bhima had stolen my lines. He stood there beaming as Virata and Chekitana smiled, and the tension in the tent was gently sucked out.

Dhristadyumna continued, 'I thank the council for its belief in my ability, though I must admit, there is already a plan.'

Now it was Drupada's turn to beam. 'Of course there is! Tell us, how are we going to wipe them out today?'

Dhristadyumna looked embarrassed and glanced at Krishna uncomfortably as he spoke. 'It's not entirely mine…'

He cleared his throat and continued, 'My belief is that either Drona or Radheya will command the troops today. My analysis is that none of them will try the *chakravyuha* again because they played their gambit yesterday by drawing Arjuna away from the main formation. Krishna had the same feeling…uh… Would you like to…,' he indicated to Krishna who smiled at him and took the thread of conversation from his fumbling hands.

'My lords, as Dhristadyumna pointed out most astutely, they are probably not going to use the *chakravyuha* again. Now, I'm not an expert in battle tactics, which is why Dhristadyumna had to put my thoughts together in war terms, but the gist of it is this—today, we shall give them Arjuna. Serve him on a platter for them.'

The council was stunned. Dhristadyumna piped in. 'Er… what he means to say is…just for today, we shall create a unified force…not dividing it like yesterday…and have Arjuna lead in the van. We've devised a modified *garuda* formation where Arjuna with his Indraprastha contingent will be at the beak, and the Matsyas and Panchalas will be at the wings. Chekitana, you can bring up the rear.'

'Matsyas will be at the rear today. I can't expose them to two consecutive days of hard fighting,' squeaked Virata. His voice had become shrill over the past few days with the exertions of screaming in order to be heard on the battlefield. He now either shrieked or squealed in conversations.

Dhristadyumna sensed the tone and said, 'All right, my lord, Chekitana, will you take up the wing with us?'

Chekitana shrugged, a little embarrassedly.

Drupada bouldered in, 'Why should the Matsyas get an easy day? Weren't the Panchalas in the thick of it too? We should get a day at the back, son.'

'Nonsense, all the Panchalas are doing is hunting Drona for their king's petty revenge, and that too, not very successfully,' responded Virata sharply. 'We need to bring this war to a swift conclusion. I've stretched my men and resources to every possible limit, and I'm afraid we can't go on for much longer. This war has already gone on for thirteen days and today will be the fourteenth.'

'I'm glad you haven't forgotten how to count. Maybe what you need is a lesson in how to fight,' said Drupada, bristling. I winced. Tact had never been one of Drupada's virtues but Virata had just lost his son-in-law.

'I don't need a Panchala to teach me! Your troops have spent thirteen days and still haven't been able to get Drona. Not even when he's right under your noses,' screeched Virata.

'We can settle this outside, you and I. No need for our troops to get involved,' said Drupada, clenching his fist.

'I will put you over my knee and spank you!'

'My lords,' said Krishna firmly, 'we have an entire day's battle ahead of us. It would be prudent if we spent our anger on the Kaurava troops. Remember, it's they who are the enemies; none of us need new ones. No one for a moment doubts the bravery of the Panchalas or the Matsyas. But I think we all agree that we need to end the war quickly and for that we need our best troops in the front. Lord Virata, you may be best served in the reserve today but I doubt it will be easy. You may see your troops come into play sooner than you think. Our forces have thinned drastically from yesterday as your own quartermasters will probably tell you.'

I felt very tired. Drupada and Virata had been at it since the beginning of the war. Each felt the other wasn't contributing enough to the cause. None of us could get involved in their arguments since we were all much younger. As Drupada's sons-in-law, we could not possibly take a stand against him. On the other hand, Virata's contributions were substantial and we couldn't afford his walking out either. So, the five of us would normally sit in silence hoping for someone else to gently distract them away from their anger, back to more constructive topics of conversation.

Dhristadyumna and Shikhandi mercifully did not take sides and neither did Satyaki and Chekitana. The onus of negotiating peace between the two therefore fell on Krishna who was neither an immediate family member nor a total outsider and could provide a balanced opinion. Drupada and Virata glowered at each other but said no more.

Dhristadyumna continued without looking at his father, 'Krishna is…er…right. I want to take the Panchalas into one wing. Chekitana will take the other.'

Drupada shook his head and pleaded, 'My son, if we lose all our troops on this field, we won't have any to defend the kingdom.'

Dhristadyumna looked uncomfortable and didn't know

what to say. None of us did. No one had expected the war to go on for as long as it had. Again, it was Krishna who came to the rescue. 'My lord, if all goes according to plan, the Indraprastha contingent at the van will take the brunt of the offensive. You have nothing to worry about. Dhristadyumna, please continue with your explanation.'

Dhristadyumna paused, still wrestling with the image his father had put in his head. He unfurled a map of animal hide and put it on a table. All of us dragged our chairs closer to it. The map contained the day's formation and troop positions.

'Er...yes...there will be two parts to this formation. The first—the offensive part denoted by the beak and neck—will be led by Arjuna and supported by Bhima, and the second—the defensive part—is where...er...Chekitana and the Panchalas will come into play. The beak will pierce the centre of the Kaurava formation. If it is a *chakravyuha*, Arjuna will be able to negotiate it since he knows how to, and if it is not, well, er...it will still be effective against most formations. The beak will be supported by Bhima, and I will be at the neck.'

'The spies are telling us all sorts of things, but I feel it's... er...not prudent to trust them after yesterday. The *garuda* is a versatile formation. If Arjuna gets overwhelmed, the beak and neck will collapse into the wings that are reinforced with more troops. Between our two wings, we will be able to hold off any attackers.'

Krishna stood up and Dhristadyumna let him continue. 'We'll put the best chariot warriors of the Indraprastha contingent in the beak which will be supported by Bhima and Ghatotkacha, along with his tribal contingent. Dhristadyumna will be at the base of the neck. Shikhandi and Chekitana will command one wing, and Lord Drupada, the other, with Nakula and Sahadeva. Yudhishthira, you will be at the back again today with Virata. I don't think Drona has given up on you.'

At the back, again. No surprises there.

Dhristadyumna took up the speech. 'Morale is low in our camp. No one has seen anything like the *chakravyuha*. The soldiers feel Radheya is some kind of tactical genius and...'

'...which is why, it is probably best for Arjuna and Bhima to be in front today with the troops. To show our best warriors still lead from the front,' Krishna completed Dhristadyumna's point. A good thing too, my brother-in-law would have taken a yuga to get there. The nonchalance with which they spoke about using Bhima or Arjuna never failed to astonish me, although I was somewhat used to it by now. Did they really think Bhima or Arjuna were invincible? Or that they were much better than any other soldier? They were good warriors, no doubt. Drona always used to boast that they were the best in Bharatvarsha, but had he really seen each and every one of them? No one had known about Radheya till that archery tournament in my eighteenth year.

No one had known about Abhimanyu till yesterday.

I looked at Arjuna who appeared to be talking to himself. No one else seemed to be worried. Krishna spoke to him in between interacting with the other council members. That relieved me. I always felt the bond between those two was stronger than what I had with him. Still, I felt it was my duty to look out for him.

'One last thing. Yudhishthira, Satyaki will be with you. He fought hard yesterday, so we'll give him some rest today.'

I cringed when Krishna asked Satyaki to stay with me.

Satyaki was a prince from the Yadava confederacy who we had gotten to know through Krishna. He was one of the best warriors on the field, but totally self-obsessed. He could not stop talking about himself, or something else equally inane. He did not know the concept of following a pattern in a conversation.

One moment he would talk about ancient war techniques, the next he would expound on butterflies, completely oblivious to the fact that someone else was trying to converse on a single topic with him. He was unfailingly cheerful: one of those men who were always in high spirits, unencumbered by the empathy to tone down the exuberance of his mood when the others around him were in a more contemplative mood—as I often was.

The sabha was wrapped up and we headed back to our respective tents to get ready for war. Bhima walked some of the distance with me. He was in a better mood than last night.

'Ghatotkacha and I. It's a good day. Can't say I'm overly happy about having him so close to the front but I suppose the boy has really distinguished himself. I mean, how many boys of his generation stand in the van or even close by?'

Bhima was right. Our own sons were normally kept in the reserves to dip their toes in blood but never to get fully immersed, except the most exceptional ones who were being groomed for generalship or kingship. My own boy with Draupadi, Prativindhya, spent most of his time in the reserve. I hadn't seen him for four days but I knew he was all right. Vishakha, my retainer, updated me regularly about him.

I felt a sudden urge to see him. To hold his face between my palms and feel his skin against mine. There was little time now, so I resolved to meet him today after the battle. We each had one child with Draupadi, and unlike Bhima and Arjuna who had taken other wives, I had moored myself only to her.

The sound of Bhima's rambling brought me back to the present. '...Indravarman, the chief of the Malavas, had a tusker he wanted put down. Wretched beast had taken a spear in the throat and was in terrible pain. He was too fond of the elephant to do what was necessary so I killed the beast for him. Splendid creature. His name was "Ashwatthama". I laughed so hard when I heard the name...'

I mentally blocked Bhima's voice and smiled indulgently at whatever he said till I reached my tent. Vishakha stood outside, looking worried. Something was wrong. As soon as I came within earshot, he got straight to the point, 'Prativindhya, sire. They can't find him.'

GHATOTKACHA

AMMA NEVER TIRED of telling me the story of how she and Appa met.

Appa was a young prince at the time and entered the forest during his travels with his mother and brothers. My uncle, Hidimba, was the chief of the forest tribes. Normally, he would deal with all encroachers by getting his men to slaughter them at sight. This time, however, his pride got the better of him. When he saw that my father was as tall and as broad as him, he wondered whether he could beat him in a wrestling contest. And soon, instead of ordering his hordes to kill them all, he began wrestling on the ground with Appa.

Appa won, or rather, he killed my uncle, leaving my mother, Hidimbi, alone. Amma, as usual, did the smart thing and promptly married Appa, taking control of our tribe with his help. To be fair, my uncle never treated her well and she was relieved to see his head dashed against the ground by the dark and handsome prince from the plains.

Appa left the kingdom soon after I was born but ensured that my succession to the chieftainship of the tribe was never doubted. I was established as the next chief with my mother acting in my stead till I gained maturity. The moment that happened, my mother swiftly married me off and by putting a child in my wife's belly, I ensured there would not be a vacuum in succession.

When Appa was looking for allies to secure his own kingdom, mother told me to stand by his side with a few thousand of our tribal brothers—'half an *ankini*'—in the words of this army. Of course, the opportunity to see the world beyond the forest was hardly one to be baulked at so I came along happily, leaving my wife and son in the care of my mother.

And, there was a chance to be with Appa.

Since he left soon after I was born, I only heard of him in stories narrated by my mother and other awestruck relatives. And built on these stories—these somewhat unreliable building blocks that changed shape and form depending on my mother's moods—I pieced together an image of him in my head.

When Appa asked the tribe for support, I wanted to see if that image would stand, or whether it would crumble into nothing.

I first saw him outside the army camp. He came personally to greet my brother warriors and me. He stood outside the wooden barricades of the camp, tapping his feet impatiently as our men marched slowly towards the camp. I was at the centre of our formation and all the brothers kept silent as he waded through our mass and looked at each and every one keenly. I turned my face down as I wanted to see whether he would recognize me. He walked past me, and I felt disappointed for a moment till a huge bear hug squeezed the disappointment out of me.

'My boy!' he cried, his booming voice probably startling

the camp awake.

He was larger than the man in my head that had been built by my mother's stories. More muscular too, with a huge moustache that cleaved through his face. He ate and drank as if all the food and drink in the world would end tomorrow, and laughed generously—as if all the laughter in the world belonged to him. He laughed when I told him how I resented the name he had given me before he left—'Ghatotkacha', meaning 'head like a pot', and how I kept my head bald in sheer defiance to all the teasing I faced from the rest of the forest youth. He laughed when I told him they were still afraid of him in the forest. The only time he didn't laugh was when I told him that my mother felt lonely without him. He looked away guiltily for a moment, and then returned my gaze, promising me that when this war was over, he would come back to live in the jungle for a while.

It was settled then. I would bring my father back, even if I had to deal with the rest of Bharatvarsha to do so.

When my brothers and I first entered the camp, the other men looked at us strangely and called us 'mleccha' or 'rakshasa'. 'Mleccha', I later learned was a crude word for 'outsider'. The word indicated people who did not speak Sanskrit, the dominant language of the city dwellers. It seemed the world outside had a word for everything. Even the things they knew nothing about.

'Rakshasa' was a little more complex. 'Rakshasa', I learned, were mythical creatures known to eat humans. They were short, dark, pot-bellied, and had fangs for teeth which they used to tear apart human flesh. Early on, to emphasize our 'otherness', my 'rakshasa' brothers and I set up a separate enclosure for ourselves a slight distance away from the regular soldier barracks.

This made the other soldiers suspicious of us, and we routinely heard tales about ourselves that involved cannibalism, orgies of blood and all sorts of depravities. Instead of trying to disprove any of these, we let the rakshasa stories swirl in the cups of their minds till what was left was a heady mix of untruths. Truth be told, I enjoyed the stories and the arm's length at which the rest of the army held us.

The warriors of our tribe called ourselves 'brothers'. It was an old custom of the tribe. I suppose the tribal elders, who devised such a rule, thought it was a good way to make us feel responsible for each other's lives. The method worked, for a closer set of warriors could not be found on the field. Perhaps the fact that the rest of the army did not fully trust us also brought more cohesion into our ranks.

All of us were dark and wore the robes of the jungle—thick grass and rough cloth. Most of us had never seen an armour or understood why these men walked in a straight line to battle or why they would bother creating such a wide variety of killing implements.

It was only recently that we began sleeping in leather tents, accustomed as we were to the boughs of trees and hard jungle mud. It was not an entirely unsatisfying experience in this cold land, the air of which was pregnant with the smell of carcass and burning flesh, along with the wails of humans and animals.

We did not ride horses in the jungle, preferring the company of elephants. Our skin would touch theirs as we sat on them, and we would goad them only with a few gentle thwacks of our palm. To see these magnificent beasts mounted with leather seats having not one but two drivers, who sometimes whipped them with sticks, was initially unsettling. Also, the ridiculous ritual of using conches and drums to announce battle. The sounds scared the animals, and I wondered why they were involved in a fight between humans in the first place.

While there were many things about this world that were deeply disturbing, there were also some advantages. Their bows were better, the metal sharper, and the *sura* wine lighter.

I checked my stabbing spear and hatchet once more as I prepared for the day's battle and studied the bow borrowed from my father. He had little use of it, he told me. It was an interesting thing, made of wood and animal bone, far superior to the bamboo ones we fashioned in the jungle.

Metal had reached us forest dwellers only very recently and we had scant use of it in the jungle where it was more important to hone an instinct for danger than fashion a weapon. The blades of my stabbing spear and hatchet were the only pieces of metal I had on me. Whether they were made of bronze or the new metal iron was not a detail I was interested in. They had been gifts from my mother and they hit hard and well.

My men assembled outside the enclosure and we walked to the field. My father gave me a chariot with a charioteer when we first joined the main army but I always felt uncomfortable on it. I could see the advantages of having one but I did not want to create a distinction between myself and my brothers, so I used it sparingly, more out of politeness to show my father his great gift was being used than anything else. My brothers seemed to understand this.

So the chariot followed behind us, its charioteer woeful at not having a charge like all the other charioteers. I was tempted to ask him to leave but that would have just broken his heart. In all honesty, I didn't think I would use it again.

The mud of the battleground was porous with blood and over the last few days, my brothers and I had a hard time not slipping while we fought. It wasn't just us though; chariot wheels were sinking in the bloodied ground mid-charge and elephants routinely lost their grip on the earth, occasionally stumbling and falling on their own troops.

I made my way to Appa. I had been told the army was arranged like an eagle today, though it didn't resemble one from where I stood. Appa was on his chariot though I don't think he liked it much either. My troops would occupy the centre of his formation. His soldiers opened out a hollow for us to stand and we took our positions.

'So, you're here on your feet? What's the point of getting you a chariot, son?'

'I trust the soles of my feet more than wooden wheels, Appa,' I said with a smile.

Appa beamed at me and shook his head. 'As you wish, boy. I'm not much of a chariot-man myself, but at my age, it's good to have an extra pair of legs, even if they are wooden wheels. Just keep up though.'

I smiled in acceptance. 'Yes, old man. I'll slow down for you.'

My own Sanskrit was rudimentary so I spoke to him in my tongue, which he was also well-acquainted with. Most of my orders came from him too since he was one of the very few people in the camp who could speak my people's language.

I waited for further instructions. Appa looked around and then like an excited boy, he started reciting.

Father and son get ready to fight,
Two against the Kaurava might.

*With mace and spear they will smite
and win us back our lawful right!*

Appa finished his atrocious poem, and I smiled politely as I always did, nodding vigorously without saying anything. It would have broken his heart to know his son did not think much of his skill with words.

My brothers formed up behind me, our stabbing spears ready. None of us wore armour. Armour was overrated—at least that of the common soldier which was often made of stiffened animal leather and could be pierced with a sharp blow. The trick was to strike from above and hack downwards at the shoulder since that was where the armour was at the thinnest. Bronze armour was tougher to negotiate but could be split with a few hard blows. Iron presented a more interesting challenge since it was the nature of the metal to not split.

In such cases, I told my brothers to aim for exposed body parts or try hacking at the leather straps that fastened the breastplate and back plate. This was difficult but so far, we had done a decent job.

The forest had taught us to defend ourselves through constant motion. We kept our limbs unencumbered so we could avoid blows and swing our weapons a fraction of a second earlier than our opponents. Hunters by nature, our ears and eyes were honed to pick up movement and respond instantly. Far quicker than any of these city dwellers. And it was this instinct that served us on the battlefield.

A vulture sat near my foot, pecking the ground next to it. I kicked at it and it went flying away, cawing in annoyance. The vultures had become more daring these days, as had the jackals. We could see them at the fringes of the battlefield biting the flesh of dead men, horses and elephants, tearing out their hair, licking the dried blood of the carcass or carrying severed limbs around—much like what my fellow soldiers thought I did as a rakshasa.

I looked out into the horizon. Arjuna—Appa's younger brother and my uncle—stood in front in a white and silver armour. He had a son much younger than me. A man called Abhimanyu who died yesterday. The soldiers said he was a great warrior, as great as his father. I looked at Appa, standing on the raised platform of his chariot, and wondered if he would like being compared to me.

SUSHASANA

ALL WARRIORS SHIT before battle. The ones who don't are lying. I felt a warm river snake its way down my leg and felt its wet warmth mingle with the rough leather of my sandals. Then, my bowels released their load into the seat of my dhoti. The conches blew again and the elephants moved forward. I had no time to change so I let my shit crawl down my dhoti, following the same route the river had taken.

Surmashana was a little ahead of me, on another elephant. Both armies stopped at a little distance from one another and waited for the conches to announce the precise moment when battle would commence. He took his elephant ahead a few steps and shouted to the winds. 'I am Surmashana, slayer of Abhimanyu. Where is Arjuna? Where is Bhima? Have they disappeared conveniently, like they did yesterday?'

The conches blared again and the cymbals crashed; the battle had officially begun. The drums sounded and Surmashana charged on his elephant. I spoke to the company commander on my flank. 'Send a hundred elephants behind him.'

Bhima was at the head of their formation today. I could make his chariot out, taller as it was from the others. I couldn't see Arjuna. Had the grief of losing his son overwhelmed him?

Surmashana's elephant charged ahead a few steps, and then stopped dead in its tracks and turned around, bleating horribly. A clump of arrows was stuck in its jaw, just below its head armour. The beast shook its head trumpeting and charged into the elephants I had sent out.

The leather seat mounted upon it broke and I saw Surmashana hanging from the leather strap that went around the belly of the elephant to hold the seat upright on its back. He was flung sideways and I saw his body repeatedly smack the flank of the elephant as it charged towards our ranks.

The boy held on but I didn't know what to do. My hands went numb and I began to feel giddy. I watched him struggle and prayed it would all be over soon. The elephant stopped, trumpeted in anguish and thrashed around for a few moments before falling to its knees. To my great relief, Surmashana released the strap and let himself down to the ground, tottering back into our lines.

I knew he shouldn't have gone in the van. Why did I let myself get convinced by Shakuni? He always did this to me. I made a mental note to ensure that Surmashana stayed in the reserve for the rest of the war.

An arrow whizzed past, bringing me out of my thoughts. I looked around but couldn't spot the coward who had shot at me. However, my eyes spotted a bigger prize. I saw Arjuna in his chariot driven by that Yadava, Krishna.

'Krishna, wait!' I shouted, hoping he would hear me.

He must have heard me because the coward spun his chariot away from me. I looked behind and saw Dronacharya's chariots coming up. I could make out his white armour and bow along with his battle standard of a red sacrificial altar and a black deerskin.

Time to get some work done. I took out a bow, fastened an arrow and aimed it at a Pandava infantryman. I nocked another onto the bowstring and looked around for a victim.

Krishna was taking Arjuna into our lines, supported by some other chariots in the shape of a wedge. I told my mahout to change direction and move towards him. My elephant charged and the seat shook with his motion. I almost fell over but regained my balance somehow. I lifted the bow, took careful aim and fired the arrow. It bounced off the umbrella of his chariot but got his attention. He turned towards me and I shouted at him.

'I'm coming for you!'

I picked up a javelin and flung it at him with all my strength. His chariot swerved and my spear got stuck in the mud. I picked up another one and took careful aim again, but his chariot refused to stay still. Finally, a group of soldiers blocked his chariot's path and it slowed to a halt. I took aim again and threw the javelin. It smashed the side of the chariot and dented it.

'Hey Krishna, since you're afraid, tell your boy to fight!'

Arjuna turned around, and before I could lift another spear, he let three arrows loose. I ducked and the first two flew above my head. The third one caught my shoulder plate but didn't even tickle me.

'That was lucky! Try again!' I roared but to no avail. The chariot fled away from the fight.

'Chase him,' I told my mahout. The mahout goaded my elephant which trampled through the lines. The chariot gained momentum and sped away. I roared once again but to no avail. They were gone.

I was at a little distance from my elephant company that was engaged with the Pandava front line. There was no time to go after him. I ordered my mahout to take us back. A cluster of spearmen gathered around and tentatively poked at my beast. The mahout tried to get the beast to tusk them but the stupid animal refused to do so. A peace-loving wild animal? This was a first. I picked up a javelin and threw it at the nearest spearman. It caught him between the shoulder and neck and skewered him like a pig. Then, I had a better idea. I removed my dhoti, soiled as it was, swung it around and threw it on another spearman's face.

The poor man did not know what hit him. I tried to make out his expression as he peeled off my stinking cloth bag of shit that clung to his face. The next moment, he had disappeared under a mass of spearmen who took his place. I don't think any of them noticed a half-naked man wiggling his penis at them from atop an elephant. I quickly wrapped another dhoti which I always carried as spare. Battlefields were full of sharp objects and having spare clothes never hurt anybody.

GHATOTKACHA

THE NAKED MAN on top of the elephant was either very brave or very foolish to expose his privates when so many arrows were flying around. Anyway, I did not have time to speculate the nature of his pride. The eagle's beak, as Appa called it, needed to penetrate deeper into the Kaurava line, but for some reason it was not being able to. Appa and I came in to support Uncle Arjuna and his contingent as they fought their way through.

Uncle Arjuna was a fine warrior. Some said that he was perhaps better than Appa though I don't think the two could be compared. While Appa was better on the ground and in close combat, my uncle was better at a distance. But what an eye! I had heard stories that he could down a parrot by shooting it through its beak, or its eye—I couldn't remember exactly—while it was hidden within the green of a tree. I could believe it too. He didn't seem to take a moment to find his target and took even less time to pick up an arrow from the quivers arranged in a criss-cross pattern within his chariot. When a quiver got empty, he merely tossed its corpse outside his chariot to join the mass of human ones.

My reverie was cut short by an arrow that nicked my arm

and drew blood. I looked at the direction from where it had come to see the offending party. It was my father's old Guru. Throna, I think that was his name, though my father told me he used to call him Acharya or Guruji as a student. I don't think he was aiming for me specifically though; Throna was scattering arrows everywhere as his troops surged into our lines.

I whistled to my brothers and they closed up behind me. The Kaurava foot soldiers were breaking through the thin layer of my father's troops and had almost reached us. From the corner of my eye, I saw Throna manoeuvre his chariot into Uncle Arjuna's path. Uncle Arjuna's charioteer, also a great favourite of Appa, swerved his chariot out of the way and avoided battle. Soon, Throna was surrounded by our foot soldiers and got busy slaughtering them.

I was being crushed—by my brothers from the back and Appa's troops from the front who were breaking their line even as the Kaurava foot soldiers poured into them. My stabbing spear, short as it was, was of no use here. I removed my hatchet and began to hum. Behind me, my brothers began to hum too. The last soldier in front of us got cut down and my brothers and I went forward, swinging our hatchets.

I was being pressed forward by my brothers. I gripped the hatchet tightly in my hands. It was a short one, no longer than the distance between the top of my middle finger and my elbow. We normally wielded two of them together, but in close quarters, it was better to have the second hand free to push away opponents.

A sword was thrust at me; I danced out of its way and slashed my assailant across the face. With the same motion I brought my hatchet-wielding hand down and slashed another man across his neck. In such close proximity to the enemy, every blow needed to be a killing one, and no swings could be wasted. My brothers swarmed up behind me and we began repelling the Kaurava assault.

It was not an easy fight. The Kauravas gave as good as they got. Over the past thirteen days, they'd learned that the only way to counter the brethren was to team up and attack them simultaneously from opposite directions. More than once, our brothers had been killed because of injuries on both sides of the body. Appa came up from behind in his chariot with a ring of archers and foot soldiers wielding maces to bring up the line. The foot soldiers joined my brothers and we pushed the Kauravas back towards their chariots while the archers furiously fired at us. Appa got off his chariot and jostled his way next to me.

I couldn't actually see him, focused as I was on avoiding an oncoming blow. But I could sense him, his footsteps heavier than my brothers.

He was right behind me now and I ducked, sensing his mace swing above me. Its huge round head smashed the skull of the man in front of me and I scythed the knee of a soldier who tried to attack Appa from the side. I swung and took my position behind Appa's shoulder. My brothers fell behind, and Appa and I alternately smashed and hacked a circle around us. The Kaurava troops backed off a little and approached us warily. The mad bloodlust of the first few moments was gone. Like wolves, they realized they needed to be cautious of their prey. Appa grunted in my ear. 'We need to create a path for Arjuna. He's behind us.'

I could feel the rumble of chariot wheels beneath my feet. He wasn't far behind. I raised my free hand and made a fist;

my brothers formed a crescent behind Appa and me. The wind built in my chest and I began to hum. A low drone at first that rose to a crescendo. My brothers joined me, and soon, in between all the hacking and maiming and killing, we began to sing.

Songs gave us courage. They helped us block out the carnage around us and focus our energy on killing. We sang as we fought because we believed that if our souls were released while we sang, they would go to the heavens, borne on the wings of musical notes.

The men sang in rhythm from behind and we charged into the Kaurava troops who were standing still. Appa ran ahead of me as I picked out the stabbing spear from the satchel slung behind me and thrusted it into a soldier's thigh. Then I decapitated him with my hatchet and yanked the spear out simultaneously. The next few moments were spent whirring around, avoiding blows. A sword slashed the skin of my wrist but Appa's mace came down on the culprit. It stung, so I sang louder to quell the pain. Appa looked indulgently at me.

'I knew I had chosen well with your mother the moment I heard yours was a singing tribe. We'll sing one of my poems in your language one day,' he said, very seriously. As much as I did not look forward to singing father's poetry, the thought secretly delighted me. Hopefully, some day soon, we would sing together in the forest with Amma listening. The rumble of the chariots got heavier on the ground and we parted ways as a hail of arrows signalled the arrival of Uncle Arjuna.

ARJUNA

THE CHARIOT IS moving and I appear to be moving with it. My body parts act on their own volition. My hand stretches down and fetches three arrows from a quiver. One arrow, I clench between my teeth, the second one is grasped by my hand that's stretching the bowstring, and the third one gets nocked onto the bow.

You never really cared for this method, did you son? Always preferred less complications. The truth is, son, simplicity is overrated, especially when it comes to solving problems. Complexity shows depth of thinking. The simplest thing to do is to pick up an arrow and aim at an adversary. But the motive of shooting an arrow is to end a war quicker, and hence, to kill as many people as quickly as possible. Therefore, it is imperative to devise a system that enables you to do so, even if it is at the cost of some sanity. Clarity of purpose, son, that's what makes a warrior good or bad, and a solution, simple or complex. Most warriors pick a purpose that is immediate—killing the man in front of them—rather than looking at the larger picture and acknowledging its complexities.

Take the man in front of me. A man called Achyutayus. A

minor king in the Kaurava faction who I remember from our time at Indraprastha. He's counting on one arrow to kill me. He ponderously picks it up, takes aim, and I've already dispatched three at his head and neck knowing at least one will make the mark. All three do. Two in the neck, one through the forehead. He snakes to the floor and his charioteer carries his dead body back to his lines. The lesson is, he who puts more into the fight wins it. Clarity of purpose.

Dronacharya comes in front of me and your uncle refuses to be drawn into battle with him. He takes the chariot away and I hear a thud. A javelin has bounced off the chariot's umbrella. An elephant-fighter obviously. It is Sushasana, by the looks of it. He roars something unintelligible. Krishna ignores him. I shoot off three arrows to scare him off. He's not a warrior serious enough for me to expend time on right now.

Krishna holds the reins and guides the chariot to its destination. I do nothing. I fight the people he tells me to fight and ignore those battles he ignores. I can talk to you like this only because I know that his hand is on the rein. The truth is I wouldn't trust anyone else. I know he loves me like I love him. It's a love born of instinct rather than any real strategic gain.

But I am digressing. Where was I? Sushasana is behind and Krishna has taken the chariot around. He is talking to Bhima who is looking worriedly at me, but at the same time, he is nodding. I see Bhima and his tribal son begin to carve out a path for Krishna and me. Krishna leads, I follow him into the forest of metal.

The chariot travels slowly, grinding over corpses strewn across our path like flowers. I'm picking off soldiers as they try to surround me. A belt of Indraprastha's finest soldiers gird around the chariot as it moves ahead slowly.

An arrow flies from behind, nearly taking my head off. I turn around. It is Dronacharya. The arrow was obviously meant to get my attention, that's all. Krishna looks behind and sees him; he shouts some instructions. A forest of soldiers with long spears come up between me and Dronacharya who is left protecting himself as our chariot continues to move in front.

Krishna's fellow Yadava, Kritavarma, now blocks our path with another minor princeling Srutayudha. Srutayudha carries a fat iron mace, which he picks out delicately from a leather bag. The mace is grey and has a sharp spearhead fixed on the head—a fine weapon.

Kritavarma attacks first and releases two arrows at me in quick succession. I turn sideways clumsily and allow both arrows to pass. One grazes my breastplate as it flies by. From behind me, four arrows streak towards Kritavarma. It is the Panchala princes, Yudhamanyu and Uttamaujas. They head towards Kritavarma as Krishna swerves the chariot away from him, barking instructions.

'Remove the mace from our path,' he says, tersely.

I fit three arrows and release them in quick succession. Srutayudha lifts his mace over his head and the arrows hit him at the base of his neck. His hold on the mace loosens and it falls on his head, nearly decapitating him as he falls to the chariot floor.

The men around him retreat and Krishna forces our chariot forward, surrounded by our infantry. Kritavarman is being kept in check by the Panchala princes. A row of horsemen form up in front of us. One of the horsemen brandishes a sword and calls out to me.

'Lord Arjuna, Lord Sudakshina of the Kambojas would like to have the pleasure of battling with you.'

A man on a chariot, decked in golden armour, comes from behind them. He nocks an arrow and shoots it in my direction. His aim is true as it narrowly misses my head. The horsemen give a war cry and charge towards me with their swords out. A suicide charge to buy their commander more time.

I'm not falling for it.

Three arrows. One does it for Sudakshina between the eyebrows. A glory shot if there ever was one. The other two kill two horsemen mid-charge. My infantry crowds about with their long spears and deals with the rest of them. A lancer hurtles through my infantry and misses goring me by a few inches. I nock an arrow and follow his motion as he tries to swing around for another stab. The arrow flies and hits him hard in the centre of his chest, cutting through his leather armour. He falls down and his horse canters away.

We break through a ring of soldiers or rather Krishna uses the chariot like a battering ram to push through. Krishna halts the chariot so that the foot soldiers behind us can cut a path for more chariots to join us and mount another offensive.

At a distance, stands an elephant troop led by Suyodhana who sends unarmoured men in my direction. Some of the men have golden hair. More than a week ago, I had asked Krishna how their hair was of that colour and if I could obtain it too. He had smiled and told me they were Yavanas who had come from across the seas.

I've seen people from all over Bharatvarsha, son, and they're like fruits. So many varieties, so many shapes. Long faces, big noses, small noses, round faces, black hair, grey hair, but never golden. I almost feel bad taking them down, one after another, seeing their golden hair lick the blood on the ground.

Yudhamanyu and Uttamaujas, having dealt with Kritavarma, come to my side with more Indraprastha chariots. The Yavanas never reach us. All of them are slaughtered before they can even breach our perimeter of foot soldiers. Instead, another troop of ten odd men charge at us, screaming 'Amvashthas!' Our men make short work of them too.

Krishna moves the chariot in front, and signals to the others to form in a line. There are twelve or thirteen of us that face Suyodhana. Krishna stands up on his seat and takes out his conch. He points at Suyodhana and speaks loudly to our line.

'On my count, charge.'

SUSHASANA

My elephant was injured. It kneeled to the ground and refused to stand up. It kept shaking its head and trumpeted loudly. I cursed the useless mahout and kicked him for good effect before I jumped off the beast's back and got on my chariot that had been following the elephant.

I saw Guruji had not been able to penetrate the Pandava lines. There was a group of chariots huddled around him, trying to push through. The elephants had clearly been unsuccessful in making a path for him. I told my charioteer to join him. He was talking to Suyodhana who was looking angry.

'There's no point complaining. The elephants did not break through. If you had directed them like I told you, we would not be stuck here. It will be mid-day in some time. Now the chariots have to do the business,' said Guruji calmly.

'It's always something with you, Guruji. We're never good enough. Not like the Pandavas. The elephants had created a gap but the chariots weren't there to take advantage of it.'

I stepped in and added my lines. 'The elephants had done their job. I was there. My own got injured in the melee.'

Guruji never rated me, so he ignored my comment.

'There's little time. Let me take the chariots and set up a charge. Send Kritavarma and the Narayanis behind and follow them up with the Leopard Guard, and maybe Jalasandha too.' He looked a little tired, but now was not the time for him to be tired. There was much fighting to be done.

I took up my position with Guruji who continued to ignore me. The conches blew and our chariots tried charging through the lines of spears in front of us but didn't get very far. Guruji started shooting arrows and immediately, a few spearmen fell to the ground. The chariots next to Guruji also started shooting arrows and some space was created in front of him. He charged into it and broke through the Pandava line. We followed his trail closely with foot soldiers running behind us to create a wider opening. The Pandava line melted away into retreat as more of our chariots joined in the fray.

Our men were now arriving in great force. Kritavarma and his Narayanis came on a chariot in perfect order as usual, in their yellow dhotis and dark blue armour that was embossed with a plough insignia. Jalasandha, a minor ally of ours from god knows where, came in with his troops in green attire. Together, they looked like a massive metal peacock. I joined Kritavarma's troop. It was always fun to fight with the Narayanis. They made fighting so easy, even if Kritavarma was a bit of a stick in the mud.

'You had an elephant troop...a hundred, right? Where?' He demanded, the moment he saw me.

I looked at him coldly and did not reply. He sighed loudly, shook his head disapprovingly, and turned to face the Pandava line. His chariot lurched ahead. I waited for a few moments till his troop had passed and fell in behind them, at a slight distance.

A Broken Sun ≈ 59

Jalasandha's troops formed in behind us in a tidy line, though without the finesse of the Narayanis. I looked behind and in the horizon, I could see the very end of our army. I looked forward and could see the last lines of Pandava troops not very far from where we were. Both armies had thinned but we still had more soldiers. It looked like the reserves of both armies would fight today.

Vinda and Anuvinda joined me. They were the twin kings of Avanti who were distantly related to us. I could not tell them apart. They were identical twins who wore identical armour and fought with identical bows and arrows. Sometimes, they even completed each other's sentences which never failed to amuse me. They ruled the Avanti kingdom together in much the same way. I had never heard them contradict each other, so it may have been possible. Two men sharing the same mind. I wondered if they also shared the same woman.

I don't think I would have been able to. Not even with Suyodhana, forget any of my other half-brothers, which as per the last count before the war, was a hundred according to the bards. Honestly, I had no idea about how many sons or daughters Father had. There was Suyodhana with Gandhari-ma, but the rest of them, like Vikarna or the worm Yuyutsu, were necessary outcomes of alliances or because my father felt particularly lustful one evening.

Our family has always secured its interests through marriages. Most families do in Bharatvarsha, but Father made it a fine art. Most of our troops today came from marriage alliances or relations and if our army was the largest in the world today, forget Bharatvarsha, we had him to thank for it.

He is a distant father though. Who wouldn't be if he had

to divide his attention among a hundred children? Assuming the bards are off even by fifty children, that's still fifty brats.

I myself only knew of seventeen.

Seventeen children, and by that extension, seventeen wives does not give you much time for anything else. So Father played stud bull while Dronacharya and Grandsire Bhishma effectively ran the kingdom. I suspect they liked it that way. Guruji was master of the Gurukul and supreme marshal of the forces, and Grandsire took care of the other stuff—alliances, irrigation and the other boring bits.

I don't think they were happy when Yudhishthira claimed the throne and offered to take the burden of governance from them. I think they preferred Suyodhana who liked having the title of king but did not really care for the responsibilities. Maybe that kind of power appealed to them. I don't know why it would though.

After the Pandavas were banished for thirteen years, no one expected them to make it back. The kingdom was running well with Grandsire, Guruji and Suyodhana not interfering in each other's work.

Those were good years.

My mind returned to the battle ahead. Both Vinda and Anuvinda nodded and smiled at me as we followed the Narayanis who had begun engaging with some Pandava troops in light-blue armour.

I picked up a javelin and flung it with full force over our troops, hoping it would hit one of the enemies. It disappeared into their lines and I strained my ear hoping to hear a howl of pain. None came even after a few moments. A wasted effort. I was running out of javelins so I reluctantly picked out my bow from its holder on the side of my chariot. I took out one of the two quivers that were stored below it and strapped it to my back, looking for someone to kill.

It seemed Vinda and Anuvinda had already found someone because one of them, I couldn't tell which, nodded at me and both chariots headed away towards my left where old King Virata was fighting our troops desperately. His bodyguards were lying in their blood around his chariot and he was desperately trying to string a bow.

This would be easy.

I told my charioteer to head towards the fight. Suyodhana would be pleased if he heard I had killed one of the Pandava generals, and not just a general but a full member of their council and a king of one of the largest states in Bharatvarsha.

There was a small matter of getting to Virata before the rest. Vinda and Anuvinda were going at a leisurely pace, no doubt to stalk him first and see if it was a trap. I had no such reservations. Any fool could see Virata was in trouble. I told my charioteer to charge ahead of the kings of Avanti. We cut between them and I loosed an arrow at Virata as soon as we were at a shooting distance. The arrow bounced off the chariot as I fixed another one and took careful aim. Two arrows flew past me from either side. It seemed Vinda and Anuvinda had decided to join the fight. I shot the arrow in panic and it went over Virata's chariot.

There was more company. Alamvusha, a chieftain of the far northern mleccha tribes, came with his troop of horse archers and we surrounded the old king. Alamvusha took out an axe and began to charge at Virata. Another horseman barged in and slammed into the side of his horse. The rider was a man in black armour. He shouted 'Kuntibhoja!' and swung his sword at Alamvusha.

Alamvusha parried the first stroke with his axe. His warhorse muscled away Kuntibhoja's horse which lost its balance and nearly dropped Kuntibhoja who struggled to stay atop his horse. Alamvusha's axe rose and the next moment, Kuntibhoja's head and body had ended their brief acquaintance with each other.

Alamvusha's horse trotted towards Virata even as our arrows had begun to find their mark. An arrow of mine got stuck in the old king's thigh while Vinda and Anuvinda deprived him of a bow and maybe a finger or two. His arm was pierced by another arrow. I saw him bend down into his chariot hollow to avoid further injury.

Coward. It would all be over soon.

YUDHISHTHIRA

My fingers were cold and they wrapped and unwrapped themselves around a spear in a futile attempt to warm themselves. Prativindhya was missing. He had gone missing before—from the second to the fourth day of the battle. When I had found him on the battlefield on the fourth day, he had said he had spent the night in a tent of one of the allies. This was not uncommon. I had resisted the urge to scold him and instruct him to report to me every day. He was a warrior and we all brought our destinies like dice here in this great gambling hall of a battlefield.

I was a good father to Prativindhya, my son from Draupadi. Better than I was an elder brother I suppose. Brothers become equals in ways that sons never do, no matter how old they grow. Prativindhya was a gentle child, much like I was. He was born before our exile and we shipped him off to Mother's family in the Kunti kingdom, a part of the burgeoning Yadava confederacy being ruled from Dwaraka by Ugrasena.

Yadavas teach self-defence rather than offence so Prativindhya learned the martial arts. He wasn't bad with the bow either but he was still his father's son. He would never be as good as Abhimanyu or even Ghatotkacha, no matter how much he tried. At the beginning of the war, like all young men seeking to prove their worth, he had looked up to his uncles, Arjuna and Bhima. But soon, he found his skills lacking. I hoped that by now, he was less enthusiastic about the war, just like his father.

I had kept him away from the war as much as I could. He was assigned positions with the minor princelings in the back of the reserve. He would only fight for short durations every few days instead of taking the responsibility for winning the war. We had tried doing the same for Abhimanyu but his outrageous talent for destruction was noticed by everyone and he was rewarded with a place up front that led to his subsequent death.

I noticed that today, Dhristadyumna had wisely kept some of the younger princes in the reserve and had assigned Chekitana a position as far back as possible. I would have done the same. I hoped that Prativindhya was somewhere at the back with one of his mates. I had done everything I could within reasonable limits to protect him. To have left him entirely out of his father's war had not been an option.

I felt great weariness come over me when I thought how I had gotten my son into such a war over this kingdom. But it wasn't really about a kingdom anymore. It was about a principle. Why should the Kauravas take what was ours and bully us into relinquishing our right to it? I wasn't making sense anymore. Even to myself. I hoped Prativindhya was still alive. I would visit his tent in the evening. I had spent far too much time thinking about Abhimanyu and not my own son. Arjuna was also worrying me. But I didn't know what to do about it.

Arjuna had always been closer to Krishna than any of us. Our mother Kunti was Krishna's aunt and his father's sister.

His father, Lord Vasudeva, had wanted his son to learn statecraft from Hastinapura and growing up, Krishna had spent many months in our company. While the rest of us were always fond of his genial presence, Arjuna became attached to him. I can't say it was a bad thing. Arjuna was always quiet and after he and Bhima had been selected to attend the Gurukul for only our most talented princes, we lost the chance to build any real empathy for each other. He was my little brother and I loved him, but I could never understand him. He was closed to me and I had always been envious that Krishna saw the side of him he would never reveal to me.

From what little I had seen of him since Abhimanyu died, he had begun talking to himself. This was not strange in itself. A lot of us had taken extraordinary measures to deal with the stress of the last fourteen days. A little self-talk could not be bad. But I overheard him mentioning Abhimanyu as I walked past him into the sabha this morning. I didn't pay much attention to it then but it struck me now that perhaps he was talking to his son. Maybe the knowledge that he was dead had not dawned upon him?

I suddenly realized I had my own life to fear for. Drona was cutting through our lines as if they were lilies. I could make out that Kritarvarma and the Narayanis were at a short distance behind him. There was no one near me. Virata had gone ahead in a huff some time back to find out what was going on. This was strange considering he had insisted on staying at the back in the morning. I didn't object to his leaving as he had become exceedingly surly, snapping at anyone and anything in sight.

An arrow sailed placidly over my head. I put down my spear and lifted a javelin. It was a windless day so my aim would be true. I waited for a Kaurava soldier to come within striking distance and flung the javelin at him. It went with great speed and nearly skewered the leg of one of our own. I swore and picked up another javelin.

'Hello sir! Good day, isn't it? Splendid for blood and sunlight,' boomed a cheerful voice behind me.

He was here.

Satyaki wore golden armour and a round golden helmet along with a golden dhoti. And this was one of his less garish ensembles. He had started the war wearing purple-coloured armour, something that marked him among the troops of the enemy.

'That's the point, oh senior Pandava! Let's all get killed a little sooner?' was his reply to the accusation that he was looking to get killed. His chariot had peacock plumes around it, with a leopard pelt swung over its front. 'A little interior decoration,' in his words.

But for all his annoying habits, he was still the one warrior that Krishna counted on heavily, after Arjuna. The thought often sobered my dislike for him.

'Saw some Yavana stragglers trying to retreat from the field. Chased them down. Do you know your cousins have got golden-haired mercenaries? Why didn't we get those?'

I was too preoccupied with thoughts of Prativindhya and Arjuna to be bothered about that. I stayed silent and hoped he would lose his steam. But it was useless. Satyaki was known to talk to his enemies as he killed them, how could he possibly let a living friend off?

'It turned out they knew a mleccha tongue I'm familiar with. So I went to them and told them they had to do one thing for me if they wanted to leave the field alive. I then joined my palms and said "Namaste", and motioned them to do the same. They looked at each other, then at me, and joined their palms and said "Nah-mah-stee". I laughed so hard but made them try again. This time I bent at the hip and said "Namaste", and motioned them to do the same. You know how they said it? "Nah-mah-steeeeee". I gave them each a silver coin and told them to tuck their tails deep into their arses and never look back. I tell you, this war isn't without humour. Nah-mah-stee!'

I couldn't tell how bullying some poor mleccha to speak an unfamiliar tongue on a death threat was funny. Possibly, the poor deserters thought that Satyaki had gone mad on the battlefield just like many others. They didn't know this condition was a lifelong affliction with him.

'Drona is getting rather close. Hold on, let me send him packing. Is that okay?'

I could make out that Drona's battle standard was not very far from where I was standing. He had reached the reserves but his progress had been slowed. Satyaki commanded his chariot to go forward without waiting for my response. I said a silent prayer to the Gods for relieving me of Satyaki. His chariot filed through our troops noiselessly towards Drona.

Dhristadyumna's chariot arrived there before him with maybe a little too much haste. The charioteer could not stop the horses which cantered recklessly into Drona's red chargers. The two sets of three horses—one white, and Drona's red—got entangled with each other and thrashed around desperately to get away.

Drona had not expected this. He was holding his bow in one hand and three arrows in the other, wondering what to do next. Dhristadyumna solved the problem by unsheathing a sword and stepping gingerly over his chariot's front, onto the shoulder of his charioteer, who bore him with remarkable patience. Then, with a giant step, he stepped on one of his horses which was still struggling to get away from Drona's, but less frantically now.

Dhristadyumna stretched out on the back of the horse and put his sword sideways between his teeth. He snaked his way up to the horse's neck and then stood up, slowly and tentatively.

Drona was too surprised to respond initially. It was only when Dhristadyumna made to leap into Drona's chariot from the horse that he realized he should protect himself. He shot an arrow at almost a point-blank range as Dhristadyumna leaped into the chariot. The arrow may have glanced across his armour—I couldn't tell from the distance—but did little else to impede his progress. He fell heavily on the chariot floor as Drona jumped out of it and tried to create space between them. From the distance, I heard Dhristadyumna shout 'Wait! Wait!' as he got to his feet and lifted his sword. Did he really expect Drona to wait for him to slash him to ribbons?

Drona had regained his composure by then. He took aim for a fraction of a second and let his arrow fly at Dhristadyumna's wrist. Dhristadyumna saw the danger and brought his sword down but the arrow caught the sword and sent it spinning out of Dhristadyumna's grip. Another arrow got him on the shoulder. I saw Drona fixing a third arrow to finish the job when an arrow smacked him on the side of his breastplate. Satyaki's chariot came thundering up and Dhristadyumna took advantage of Drona's distraction to jump out of his chariot and hobble back to his own which had disentangled from Drona's.

The Narayanis came from behind and began shooting at Satyaki who decided it was in his interest to let Drona go and engage with them instead. An arrow flew in my direction and I saw Kritavarma with a group of Narayanis come at me. All of them fixed arrows in perfect unison and shot them at me. I lifted up my shield and raised it above my head as I bent into the hollow of my chariot, trying to make myself as small as possible.

The arrows fell around me. One pierced my shield but did not penetrate it. I clenched a javelin and looked up to see if anyone was within range. Kritavarma and his troops fanned out and approached me slowly. Were there instructions to take me back alive? It had to be so, otherwise they wouldn't approach me so tentatively. I gripped the javelin harder and stood up, the shield I was holding protecting as much of my frame as it could.

The Narayanis had arched their bows; I could make out seven of them. The arrows came again—this time not in an arc but in a straight trajectory. I ducked out of their range just in time. Then, as they were fixing their arrows, I picked out one of them and hurled my javelin towards him. It impaled him as he stood. My next impulse to shake my fist exultantly was curbed by six shafts flying towards me. I ducked again, just in time, but one of them grazed my arm as it passed by.

It wasn't a deep cut but a long one that made a thin path of blood along my arm. It didn't hurt much either, so I crouched into my hollow, picked up another javelin and waited for a third round of arrows.

They never came.

After a few moments of lying under my shield, I peeked out to see what the matter was, hoping they hadn't decided to charge me. They hadn't, it seemed. Four of the Narayanis could not be found upright on their chariots; my eyes scanned the horizon and saw an arrow take the fifth one in the throat. I looked up to see my saviour.

Satyaki.

Kritavarma had turned to face him. An arrow hit him on the chest and another one cut through his bow. The charioteer, realizing what was coming, turned the chariot around and drove it back towards the lines as Narayani foot soldiers covered his retreat.

Satyaki, not to be deterred, went charging right up to them and shouted, 'Nah-mah-steee!' He cackled as his chariot swerved away from their spears to head back towards me.

'That was brief. Let's go ahead and see if we can find someone else to play with, shall we?'

Before I could reprimand him on the sheer foolishness of his idea, he spoke to my charioteer. 'Behind me. Double-quick, okay?'

The rogue of a charioteer did not need any further incentive, bored as he was of sitting in one position all day. He whipped the chariot in front without asking me. I nearly told him to stop but then decided against it. If I had to fight alongside someone, it was best to do it with Satyaki who could dispatch seven Narayanis to Yama's abode in the time it took me to blink.

It was perhaps just as well that we headed out a little ahead, for we saw Virata in dire circumstances clutching his arm, surrounded by a host of Kaurava warriors. There was a wild-looking horseman who had just finished cutting down one of our warriors, possibly Kuntibhoja. Behind him were the twin kings from Avanti, and Sushasana.

I picked up a javelin and told my charioteer to head towards the fight. I thought I saw the impudent wretch grin as he picked up the reins and whipped them. Satyaki surged ahead, drawing his bow at the same time. Two arrows crashed into the horseman who first fell off, but soon stood up dazed, got onto another horse and retreated.

Two arrows were embedded one after another into Sushasana's chest. He fell out from his chariot, but two Narayanis ran up behind him and heaved him back inside.

The twin kings turned to face Satyaki and were about to draw their bows, but stopped suddenly. I looked at Satyaki who had an arrow stuck to his breastplate. He looked perplexed as another one flew dangerously close to him, nearly taking his neck off. I could see him smile as he removed the arrow from his armour and considered his new foe.

It was Drona.

Virata's charioteer swerved the chariot around and moved it away with great speed as a band of Matsya horsemen covered his retreat. Vinda and Anuvinda followed him with a few Narayani chariots. Without asking my opinion on the matter, my charioteer whipped the horses into a gallop behind them.

'Jivaka, you could at least tell me where you're taking us,' I sputtered.

'To save Virata, my lord,' he said, as if it was the most obvious thing in the world.

I was silent as we moved quickly towards Virata whose charioteer had lost his composure, trying to escape the twins from Avanti, and was whipping the horses into a frenzy.

We weren't very far from the front line. I saw an allied flag—perhaps that of a Matsya unit—hanging limply without a breeze to stroke its chin. It was eight, maybe ten rows ahead, and beyond that, there were only enemy banners.

The troops had thinned quite dramatically over the past four days and the armies had flattened out. Where in the first ten days, one could see rows of spears up beyond the horizon, today, the horizon lay bare, devoid of wood or metal or the silhouette of man and animal. For a moment, I wanted to tell Jivaka to turn back but was paralysed with fear. If I turned back now and Virata was killed, everyone would question why I hadn't done anything—especially if Jivaka told the troops I had asked him to retreat.

I clenched the front of the chariot and gripped a javelin, looking back to see if Satyaki—or anyone—had noticed my disappearance. We went further ahead, into their lines. Virata's charioteer clearly didn't know where he was taking him, and from what I could see, Virata had curled into foetal position inside the hollow of his chariot. The twins of Avanti were following him steadily. They probably wanted to trap him within their lines and then kill him. He was as good as dead at this point.

'They seem to be taking him further inside, lordship. What should I do?' shouted Jivaka.

A javelin whooshed past me before I could reply. It fell between my running horses, nearly cutting one of them in half. I turned around. It was a man in green armour and dhoti followed by four chariots in similar attire. I gripped my javelin tightly and turned around, hoping they would lose interest in the chase after a few moments.

We were in what appeared to be the middle of the Kaurava *sakata* and it was showing no signs of slowing down. I wondered why more Kauravas were not stopping us. Maybe we didn't represent a dangerous enough threat. I had no time to ponder over it for Vinda and Anuvinda lifted their bows in perfect symmetry and released two arrows each in quick succession at Virata's chariot. The arrows flew and missed the chariot's wheel. The chariot stopped and turned sideways.

A howl emanated from a troop of Kaurava foot soldiers who probably now realized that there were Pandava chariots in their midst. An entire company of them began chasing the chariot behind Vinda and Anuvinda. Not to be outdone, Jivaka whipped the reins and tried to move parallel to Virata's chariot before the Avanti kings or the foot soldiers got to him. Another javelin fell a few feet behind my chariot as the warrior in the green armour and his chariots came closer behind me.

Virata's chariot stopped. The charioteer had been shot through with arrows. A great whoop could be heard as a group of horse archers approached the chariot and began circling it. This was it for Virata. I could do nothing more. Jivaka still moved the chariot boldly towards him.

'We're being chased,' he shouted. I looked to see the chariots with the green attired warriors nearly parallel to us on both sides. I picked a stabbing spear and braced myself to lunge. The warrior on my left was closer, so I stabbed him, but missed. He held a mace which he was waiting to use on me.

He never got the chance.

An arrow flew at him and he spun out of the chariot. Jivaka whipped the horses again and we overtook the chariots with the men in green armour. I looked ahead, hoping that the arrow which had removed my pursuer had come from a benevolent source. I was not disappointed.

Arjuna was in front, just a little distance away, with a horde of our Indraprastha chariots. They were heading towards Virata's chariot and he had already begun duelling with Vinda and Anuvinda. I was about to raise my hand and shout to get his attention when an arrow nearly took it off. I turned around and pulled out a javelin from a quiver to aim at one of the green armoured men who I thought were still chasing me, and saw they had slowed down and were already a small distance behind me. Another chariot came into view and overtook them.

Drona.

The next moment, an arrow struck me in my chest and my knees gave way.

ARJUNA

THE REAL REASON the Kauravas and their allies are having such a tough time winning this war, son, is that the nature of the soil has changed. Despite the sun's best efforts, fourteen days of relentless bloodletting has transformed what was previously a barren wasteland to a pulpy reddish-brown mess that is relentlessly being churned by the feet of horses and men. I also suspect the battlefield has shifted a little to the right since we've all made a conscious attempt to stay clear of the centre where the ground is now slushy and uneven. Chariot wheels are sinking in the mud, elephants are losing balance, men are slipping and getting trampled over as they lie. All in all, it is a very nasty business. It's bad enough having to watch your back from the enemy, you also have to now know what's beneath your feet.

Over the last couple of days, the scavengers and body collectors have also given up, so there are thousands of dead bodies just lying on the field. Some of them have even been stacked in towers, forgotten by the collectors of the dead. Weapons lie on the battlefield, forgotten and devoid of purpose, like toys strewn carelessly by children after playing with them.

To Krishna's credit, he seems to avoid these rather well, and while the ground gets bumpy at times, it rarely affects my shot.

Virata is lucky to be alive. I remember hearing that he was supposed to be near the reserves today. Maybe I am wrong. I've not been myself lately, son. But you don't have to worry. I'll be fine. There are some journeys a man must make alone.

Vinda and Anuvinda are good archers. There seems to be some sort of telepathy between them, just as there is between Krishna and me. Our chariot turns around to face them sideways—so that I have a wider shot. They shoot four arrows at the same time, fletched by the feathers of a heron. When shot, these arrows hiss in the wind giving the effect of a snake coming with great speed. A good trick to intimidate inexperienced or mleccha warriors. Just who do they think I am?

Twin fighters are always difficult to kill. Most of the time their thought processes are finely tuned and they are able to cover up for each other's inadequacies. However, there is a way to kill them. You see, in every pair of twins, there is always a 'thinking' one. The man, or woman—for I have encountered them as well—who acts a fraction of second before the other. It's almost never evident who this one is since they attack with great rapidity, but Guruji—back when he was still my Guru and not my enemy—taught me a way once. You look for the twin with the longer draw of the bowstring. Since he is controlling the pair, he has more time to draw his bow, the other one draws his bow just a fraction shorter.

Before the arrows reach me, I know the one on the left is the thinking one, though I am not sure if it is Vinda or Anuvinda. Regardless, I duck and let the arrows fly over me, hissing like irate snakes. I then stand up and fire three arrows at different heights—the head, stomach, and groin—at him. The twin tries to duck, but one of the arrows catches him deep in the thigh. The other twin glances at him for just a moment and I take my chance and fire three arrows in rapid succession. Each of them strikes his neck and his head bobbles off, falls onto the chariot floor and then rolls unceremoniously into the mud. The other twin wails and I waste no time sending him to our maker with an arrow in his forehead.

A few warriors in green armour surround me. I recognize their king, Jalasandha, though I don't remember which kingdom he is from. Somewhere close to Magadha, I think. He looks at me and nods. There are so many of these familiar strangers lurking around in the battle. I pretend not to recognize him and Bhima saves me from a potentially awkward situation. He comes up, leading a chariot corps. They halt when they see us. He then brings his chariot close, sees Jalasandha and takes out his mace from its leather cover. No words are exchanged but Jalasandha nods and tells his men to stay away as he takes out his own. The chariots huddle around to form something resembling a circle, and both Bhima and Jalasandha occupy the uneven ground between the chariots.

I don't like things in irregular shapes. A duelling pit should be round, not a jagged polygon between chariots. Krishna thinks I have a need to exert control on every little aspect of my life. I can't disagree.

Mace duels rarely interest me despite Bhima's enthusiasm. More often than not, they lead to a lot of unnecessary bloodletting. The fights themselves are so slow. I am tempted to move on but decide against it to protect Bhima if someone tries to change the rules of the duel.

In this event, the fight doesn't take very long. The green armoured Jalasandha swings, Bhima leaps away, swings back and smashes his mace into the side of Jalasandha's head. The king totters and stumbles into Bhima's mace that swings with greater force the second time. Jalasandha falls and does not move. His soldiers circle around and lift his lifeless frame delicately towards a chariot.

I hear Krishna's voice. 'Drona!' he shouts, and manoeuvres our chariot away from him. I can see why. We have a chance to reach the heart of their reserves and flank them. At this point, there is no sense in being distracted by Drona. Some of the Indraprastha chariots circle around us, forming a barrier between Drona and me. Yudhamanyu and Uttamaujas along with a few others form a wedge and we forge ahead. Progress will be be slow from now. Our soldiers are getting tired and the reserves are fresh and will fight with more energy.

Ashwatthama comes up from the front. He is on a chariot and leads a company of foot soldiers who plant themselves on the ground, remove bows and begin lifting arrows. Krishna sounds the charge and we scatter them even before they have time to release their first wave of arrows.

Ashwatthama is not going to give up. His chariot stands still even as the men around him run. He sends one arrow that nearly takes Krishna's head off and another crescent-headed one that nearly hits my arm. I am about to return fire when his chariot wheel sinks into the mud. His horses try to pull the chariot out of the mud but the wheel breaks and Ashwatthama goes flying out. He nearly lands beneath the legs of the chariot horses next to him. I see him stand up and totter about a few moments later. He does not look badly injured.

We make our way further into the enemy lines and break through the *sakata*, only to be confronted by the reserve army, arranged as a *chakravyuha*, a little distance ahead. We cut our way through the main army with more than an hour of sunlight left to do what we please with the reserves. Krishna stops our chariot and lets someone else lead the van.

'Horses are thirsty' is all he says and takes out three leather pouches of water that he has kept in store for them. I get off and stand next to him with my bow ready. It isn't really necessary since we are surrounded by our own chariots. But it is good to finally stretch my legs. I walk over to him and as the horses drink the water, he looks at me and smiles kindly.

'Make your peace with him,' he says.

That is our conversation. I fear it's longer than most I've had with you, son. The knowledge of this sparks suddenly and violently. My knees buckle and I sit down on the ground soaked with the blood of a stranger. I know you're here next to me. I can smell you in the air through the fire and death. It is the fresh scent of a newborn. The smell comes back to me from twenty years ago—the first time I had lifted you and inhaled your being into mine. I remembered that smell last night and it hasn't left me since.

I know I wasn't there. For thirteen years, and then yesterday, for the final time. But you've still come back for me. I'm not sure I can thank you enough.

Krishna's finished giving water to the horses. Let me inhale your scent once more and get back to work.

GHATOTKACHA

THERE IS A saying in our parts—the jungle lets live both those who eat leaves and those who eat animals.

I saw Uncle Yudhishthira fall back into his chariot. Even this, he did with grace. Like a lotus collapsing into water. It would be sad to see him die. He wasn't a fighting man like Appa but not everyone has to be. The jungle was big, but the world was small and often herded men into doing things they couldn't do, simply because there was no one else to do it.

Uncle Yudhishthira did not want to be king. But the world had decreed he must—for the sake of order, for the sake of continuity, for the sake of god knows what.

I saw him trying to get up from the chariot. There was still life in him. I detached from our main troop with a company of brothers and headed towards him. I was not the only one who had that idea. My uncles, Sahadeva and Nakula, turned their chariots and rushed towards him too. My brothers and I formed a barrier between Throna and Uncle Yudhishthira.

Throna decided not to pursue the matter. He didn't have too many troops at hand and more of our troops were entering the fray. He quickly turned the chariot around and left. A small contingent of our chariots followed him, hoping to isolate and kill him. Uncle Yudhishthira was taken out of his chariot and put into Uncle Sahadeva's, which then went back towards our lines.

What was he doing out here? And were the Kauravas so careless that they let him through knowing who he was? I looked at Uncle Yudhishthira's chariot that had arrows all over it, its battle standard cut off. Perhaps they didn't know who he was. He had spent most of battle in reserve and without the battle standard, there was little to distinguish him from the other chariot warriors that rode across these fields.

Another thought struck me. Had the Kaurava allies reached our reserve? Was Uncle Yudhishthira escaping them? I looked behind and saw their battle standards mingling with ours in the distance. If they had broken into our reserves, the only way we could counter it would be to break into theirs. Or make the great leap trying.

There is a custom in our jungle. When boys reach an age they can be looked upon as men, there is a rite of passage we must perform. Deep in the forest, in its darkest heart, there is a hill the city dwellers call Aranyaka. We don't have a name for it for we know it's older than us. No child names its parents, after all. This hill is like a deity for us. On the day we are told we have become men, we have to climb the hill and reach the top. From the top, we must take the great leap. On the slope of the hill, there is a precipice that juts out towards another precipice a few feet away. Every child must leap from one precipice to the other. It's not a very big jump though it can be a challenge for some of the smaller children. But I haven't heard of any child not making it. There are many shrubs below to break anyone's fall. In real terms, the leap isn't that much. In symbolic terms, it's another story.

The great leap is a promise to the earth that we are responsible for our deaths from that day on, that we will seek protection from no one else, and decide the time and manner of our end—the great leap into the inscrutable darkness of the after life—on our own. We all take the great leap. If we're lucky, we get to choose the hour for ourselves.

It seemed Uncle Yudhishthira was not going to be forced to take his leap today.

SUSHASANA

That whore's son's arrows had splintered my armour but hadn't penetrated it. It took me a few moments to regain my senses and the next thing I knew, Virata's chariot had disappeared. I cursed the bastard who had shot me. This had been my best chance for glory yet. No one would have ever called me a boor or an oaf or a fool had I killed him.

I looked around and saw Guruji exiting from the front line and charging back into our lines. Kritavarma was now heading the attack joined by our Leopard Guards. It was always great fun to watch the Leopards with their colourful pelts and synchronized attacks. They would plant their feet and swing their axes upwards and downwards in a fluent motion. I had never seen them break formation and it was very hard to defeat them as the Pandavas had learned over the past few days.

They were the best troops I knew, marginally better than the Narayanis in my opinion though I would never say it to Kritavarma who was very prickly about the quality of his troops. He was like those artists who are forever defensive about their art and cannot take any criticism. Only his art was war. If you told Kritavarma that his formation was a few degrees awry he would shout at you and call you a liar. He took great pride in organizing his Narayanis, and I had to give it to the bastards—they were among the best we had ever seen.

So I let them and the Leopard Guard take care of our advance. I saw them slowly reforming into a diamond, a distinctly defensive formation that had no role for me. Guruji's retreat held more promise. He was never one to back off from a fight, so logic dictated that he was heading towards more exciting prospects.

I followed Guruji at a distance. I didn't want to get too close otherwise he would have probably snapped at me as the elders normally did. After the incident with Draupadi in the sabha, all of them had started behaving differently with me. I didn't care, of course. None of them had ever liked me. They all thought I was blindly attached to Suyodhana, just like Radheya was.

They claimed they were devoted to the Kuru cause instead of just an individual. I would often laugh at this. To be loyal to an idea, to an abstract piece of reasoning that somehow dictated how you should live your life was strange to me. Guruji's chariot picked up pace and I told my charioteer to shadow him.

Another chariot came into view a little in front of Guruji. This must have been what he was chasing. I tried making out the battle standard but it had been chopped off. I peered closely to find out the inhabitant of the chariot.

Was this an illusion?

I blinked to check my vision.

It wasn't an illusion.

Up ahead was Yudhishthira, riding alone recklessly into our lines. I didn't believe my eyes first, so I looked up again and tried to locate his battle standard. The bloody thing had been chopped off completely. But there he was, unmistakable as day. Yudhishthira, the upstart king of the Pandavas, traitor to the Kurus, riding his chariot merrily into our army with no one stopping him. I told my charioteer to hurry and looked about but there was no sign of anyone around him.

I roared at my charioteer to go faster. I would reach him before Guruji and kill him, thus ending the war within the safety of our lines. I took out my bow, tested its string and shouted at my charioteer again. A few moments of hard riding and we were inside our lines. Yudhishthira had progressed further and no one had seen him. I would talk to Suyodhana about this. Somebody's head would roll.

My horses cantered towards Yudhishthira but Guruji had too much of a lead on me. I saw him round off on Yudhishthira and shoot three arrows into his chest. Yudhishthira fell back into his chariot and I swore. This was the second Pandava leader to have slipped out of my grasp since morning. Guruji was about to move in for the kill when a Pandava contingent swarmed out and took position around Yudhishthira. Guruji realized he couldn't win this fight and turned. What I saw next horrified me.

The Pandava front line had advanced deep into our army. It seemed even Guruji was surprised that we had let them in so far. He began rallying the troops around him together and began to attack the Pandava troops. I went ahead to join Guruji to see what could be done. I couldn't see Yudhishthira's chariot anymore. He had been swallowed into their advancing force. Hopefully, Yudhishthira was dead and the Pandavas would begin to lose heart and retreat. Our troops rallied behind Guruji in the shape of a wedge. I joined them, consciously keeping out of his vision.

Guruji led our wedge into the side of the Pandava advance force where it was thinnest and our chariots broke through. I lifted my mace and smashed the skulls of two foot soldiers who were turned away from me. I saw Guruji fighting furiously, shooting arrow after arrow into their troops. The Pandava foot soldiers were already tired and began to fall away like dead leaves. Soon, we had cut the advance contingent into two halves.

I looked behind and saw Arjuna's chariot standard in the distance with a small group of chariots. I could make out Bhima's as well. They were headed into our reserve.

YUDHISHTHIRA

PRATIVINDHYA.

I gasped and came alive with his name ricochetting through my head. A sharp pain filled my chest and I coughed and groaned. For the second time, I found myself in a stranger's chariot. I tried to get up but fell back and moaned. The chariot wasn't moving for some strange reason. I tried to take a deep breath but the pain made my lungs cave in. I breathed slowly and found my equilibrium after a few moments. A worried face peered down at me. I blinked at it in response.

'He's awake. He's awake!'

Many concerned faces now crowded my sight. I recognized Dhristadyumna.

'You're…er…alive. Good.'

He didn't sound very happy. I tried to get up again but fell down. Three men picked me up by the arms and propped me up.

'I…uh…expected this from your brothers. Not you, Yudhishthira. Not you. How can we maintain the structural integrity of the formation if no one…no one…stays in their position?'

He went off in a huff. He was one to talk. Breaking off at

any given time to hunt Drona—unsuccessfully, at that. I stood up slowly, using every part of the chariot within my reach as a crutch. I couldn't tell if I was in the reserve but I didn't think so. There were troops fighting just a little ahead of me.

'Whose chariot is this?' I asked the charioteer.

'Lord Sahadeva's, my lord,' he barked.

'Where are we?'

'Near the front. The attack force has penetrated deep inside their lines. Lord Arjuna is isolated with Lord Bhima, Nakula, and my Lord Sahadeva. Lord Dhristadyumna is organizing a force that will break through them.'

Memories of the *chakravyuha* flooded back into my head. The pain in my chest rose again and I groaned loudly.

'Hello, old rose; got your thorns back, I see!'

Oh no.

'Rather brave of you, chasing after Virata. Thought I'd stop you but you looked rather set in your ways. Didn't want to hold you back. Anyway, Dhristadyumna's left me here with you, as a kind of babysitter. You know, to make sure you don't do anything naughty, like take on the entire Kaurava force on your own.'

He chuckled and looked at me indulgently. Thoughts of Prativindhya and my brothers filled my head. Was I going to lose everyone I loved today? There was a moment of utter confusion before clarity sparked unexpectedly. I didn't know if I could save Prativindhya. But I could still do something to save my brothers.

'How many men do you have with you?' I asked Satyaki.

'Twenty or thirty. Just a few Panchalas. More a bodyguard in notion than reality.'

'Dhristadyumna is mad. Using you to guard me,' I croaked. 'You should be out in front.'

'One does what one's told, old boy,' he said, chuckling.

'Let's go out in front. I need to get my brothers out.'

'No you don't. Dhristadyumna's on top of it. Besides, we can't have all of you in danger. Without you, the cause is naught,' he parroted, clearly coached by Dhristadyumna.

'Satyaki, listen to me, without my brothers, there is no cause. We won't be able to win the war if they die. The morale of the army will collapse completely. It'll be a massacre.'

I winced at the thought and continued, 'Satyaki, you're the only one good enough to break through,' I pleaded.

He was almost convinced; I could see the uncertainty in his eyes. I added for good effect. 'Only a hero can save a hero.'

He looked down and broke into a grin.

'You do lay the honey on thick, you rogue.'

'Satyaki, there is no honey. I can't sit here while my brothers are inside. Not after Abhimanyu.'

He sighed.

'Dhristadyumna's not pushing hard enough. If we set up a charge, we can probably break through. Thirty of us. Maybe create a little space for more troops, maybe even Dhristadyumna, to muscle in,' he said.

He made the chariots line up like birds in formation. Two wings. And one chariot at the head—him. I was right behind him on the left wing.

'Now, we charge, blowing our conches to give our troops ample warning to move to the side. But at no cost is anyone to stop the charge. If we trample our own, so be it. This may win us the war.'

Everyone nodded grimly. I did not agree with his tactics but I had no other plan, and Satyaki was the only one who could get me to my brothers.

Satyaki took out his conch and blew hard on it. We all joined him. I felt the pain burn through my chest as I blew again and again. Sahadeva's chariot bore me as we charged through the lines. As Satyaki predicted, our troops got out of the way of our mad dash.

But not everyone was fortunate enough. The chariots rumbled through and took down some of our own soldiers in the front line who were too busy fighting the enemy to realize that the real threat was behind them. I saw Satyaki's chariot crash through the bewildered Kaurava lines even as I blew my conch desperately. Then, I didn't have any more breaths left.

I tried sucking in air desperately but my lungs refused. My legs started shaking and the last thought that went through my head was the cold realization that thirty of us couldn't possibly help Arjuna or Bhima from the entire Kaurava reserve. I fell on the chariot floor that shook in fury as it charged.

SUSHASANA

They broke clean through our line. I could see it even though I was at a distance. Two wings of chariots crashed through our line, into the gut of our troops. Guruji saw it too and bellowed at me.

'Don't let them through. Stop the charge. Go with the Kiratas.'

A company of Kiratas assembled next to me. Suyodhana's chariot came sprinting across and overtook us. Where did he come from? He was accompanied by my son Surmashana and our brothers Vikarna, Sumukha and Chitrasena.

We pushed behind them and I noticed the warrior leading the charge was the same who had injured me earlier in the day. The one with the golden armour. This would be sweet. And this time, I had the upper hand.

Kiratas were from the mountains towards the Northeast. Hard and cold, like the wretched mountains they came from. They probably ate the rocks from the mountains too, for a hardier tribe of mlecchas I had never seen. They were slit-eyed and short, and fought with slings that they filled with stones and flung with force at the enemy. I'd seen a stone the size of a pebble go through an iron helmet a few days back. Like most mleccha tribes, they didn't care much for armour.

I told their interpreter to ready the slings as the chariots drew closer. The slingers began spinning the slings—made of rough cloth and leather—round and round to gather momentum to fling the stones they held. The chariots drew closer.

I shouted, 'Throw the stones!'

No stones flew. I looked behind to see the slingers still spinning the stones in their slings.

'Throw! Dammit!' I bellowed and looked around for the interpreter. He was slumped over. Two arrows in his belly. I gestured wildly and screamed. 'Throw! Throw!'

The chariots reached us and within moments their bowmen had cut the mountain fighters—who were still slinging their stones—to pieces. The warrior who had injured me in the morning thundered past me. I followed him and loosed an arrow that nearly took his head off. He didn't even notice it so I shot at him and missed again. I shouted at my charioteer to follow him, but he was charging at a frantic pace and we soon lost him. I looked back and saw that the Pandavas had taken advantage of the charge—they were pouring through our front lines.

I was needed there.

RADHEYA

JAYADRATHA DID NOT look well. He had drawn the short straw when it came to fighting positions yesterday and the way Arjuna and his Indraprastha chariots were charging towards us, today didn't look good either. I saw Bhima next to Arjuna. The Pandavas were really putting everything into offence today.

I took a detachment of Anga chariots with Narasimha to stop their advance. The other kings in the reserve did not show any emotion. Better his chariots than ours was probably what they thought.

We formed a crescent, halted within range of their chariots and flexed our bows. Narasimha waited till they had reached close enough and we released the first salvo of arrows. Most of the arrows missed the chariots but got a few of the foot soldiers. Our chariots moved to head them off and I found myself face-to-face with brother Bhima. He picked up his mace and stepped off the chariot.

Suta boy, *suta* boy!
Won't you come and play?
Bhima's got a mace right here
that'll turn your head to clay!

I didn't have time to get offended. I was no judge of poetry but this did not appear to be the good variety. A chariot archer of some unknown kingdom shot an arrow that missed my head; I took his off instead with a crescent-shaped one. It wasn't a clean dismembering. His head slid down his body and rolled into the mud to join its other fellow lifeless beings in the city of the dead.

A spear shaft fell hard at my feet and ended my reverie. It was a fancy one with a lapis lazuli encrusted metal shaft. Such a waste. It would likely be stolen by one of the mercenaries who would comb the field for souvenirs after the day got over or end up with the men who cleared the dead bodies.

Another javelin came swooping down at me and I jumped off my chariot as it nearly skinned me. My eyes scanned the perimeter. I saw one of the chariot warriors with Bhima picking up another javelin. I didn't take proper aim but my arrow still found the middle of his arm. The javelin dropped and taking careful aim this time, I got him at the base of the neck. He would die slowly, and uncomfortably.

Bhima was surging through, surrounded by the other Pandava foot soldiers who were more than happy to follow his massive bulk which acted like a battering ram. I wondered how they managed to make armours that big and whether it was made of iron at all.

Sujaya, one of Suyodhana's brothers, got off his chariot and rushed at him with his mace. I shouted at him to stop but he couldn't hear me. The fight was over before I could even tell my charioteer to move in that direction. Sujaya swung downwards with his mace towards Bhima's arm. Bhima took a step back and avoided the blow, pulverizing his head in the next blow.

Sujaya's helmet caved into his head, and his body in its last act, before life escaped it, slumped onto its knees.

Enraged, Sumukha rushed in his place and Bhima nearly decapitated him with a sideways stroke. Sumukha spun around and fell a few feet away from the force of the blow. His feet, I saw, had no footwear. He had been hit clean out of them. Another of Dhritarashtra's sons was dead.

No one else would die. I gathered my wits and shot an arrow straight into Bhima's chest. It probably didn't even prick him. I shot more, one after the other. He wasn't a hard target but the arrows just could not penetrate him. He smashed his way through the soldiers between us till he was in front of my chariot. This would require other means.

I took out *vatsadanta* arrows with long shafts and heads that were small and resembled a calf's tooth. I took careful aim and fired them one after another, straight in his path, just before his feet. The oaf was so engaged in pushing our troops aside like dolls that he didn't see the arrows and as I expected, he tripped over them. His mace fell a few feet away and I took the opportunity to shoot two arrows that embedded themselves into each of his arms. He yelped with pain, and I saw his troops pull him back and form a cordon before any of ours could kill him.

'Next time, fight someone of your own level. A *suta*'s too good for you,' I shouted as he was being hauled away. I didn't think he would hear me but he turned around and pushed away the men who were trying to carry him away, walking out in front. He ripped the arrows that were stuck to his arms and threw them down. He unclasped his armour from the shoulders, tore off the breastplate and leather straps, and spread out his arms. A thin, coarse cotton vest was stuck with sweat to the sharply defined contours of his body.

'If the *suta* is a man, he will wrestle me,' he roared.

I blinked and paused for a moment, not knowing how to react. This was supreme idiocy. I slowly lifted an iron arrow to put through his heart when a chariot came between us and its occupant shot an arrow straight at my head. I ducked, and by the time I looked again, Bhima had galloped onto the chariot, speeding away.

I was tempted to take aim and shoot him in the back but another arrow nearly took my head and I ducked again. I ignored it. If I got Bhima, we could win the war today.

'Bhima,' I muttered to my charioteer and he nodded and whipped the chariot ahead. Another chariot came parallel to me. It was Ashwatthama, and behind him was Kripa. They didn't meet my glance. They were here for Bhima too. We were only allies till a chance to kill a Pandava warrior of some repute presented itself. Then we became hungry dogs slobbering over a bone with scant regard for each other. I told my charioteer to steer the horses harder. If anyone would get him, it would be me—a *suta*, not these high-borns.

I looked at the other side and saw Bhurisravas behind me who acknowledged me with a nod and a wicked smile. Except for Jayadratha, we were all chasing Bhima. A maceless, armourless Bhima was not an opportunity that presented itself every day. I wondered how many chests of gold his bounty was. The same thought probably ran through the heads of all the warriors with me.

SUSHASANA

THE WARRIOR WHO had attacked me in the morning took Bhima into his chariot. I saw Radheya, Ashwatthama, Kripacharya and Bhurisravas chase him. I followed them. It would be a good way to end the day—with Bhima's death.

The chariot skidded to a stop. Ahead of it was a chariot posse with Sushaha, Sumada, Surdhara and Vikarna—my half-brothers. Their chariots closed around the warrior's chariot and prevented it from moving further. They got off from the chariot, holding maces.

This would be fun.

Some Trigarta Samsaptakas joined me, all pale in their white garb, looking like ghosts drifting along a sea of blood. Bhima stood alone with a mace that looked like a toy in his hands. He took a deep breath and charged at them, even as my brothers on the ground stood still to receive him. My chariot was coming closer from behind. I picked up a javelin and aimed between the warrior's shoulder blades, but he swivelled furiously. I steadied my javelin and waited for him to stand still, which was when I saw Bhima.

The bastard swung his mace at Sumada's face so hard that

the mace cracked. The javelin froze in my hand as I saw him kick Sushaha in the chest, pick up his fallen mace and hit him repeatedly in the head. Surdhara and Vikarna tried to attack him but their blows glanced past him, he moved so quickly.

I saw him hold Surdhara's mace as it was swung. He snatched it from his arms and then hit him in the face. Vikarna swung to hit him on the side, but overreached his swing and tipped over. Bhima took Surdhara's mace and hit him on the back of his head as he lay.

I couldn't see as tears had suddenly filled my eyes. I flung the javelin with all the force I had at him and it missed. I reached down for another javelin but realized that my stock was over. I didn't know what to do at this moment. My legs were frozen to the chariot floor. I could only watch helplessly as he stepped back onto the warrior's chariot and left.

ARJUNA

YOUR UNCLE SATYAKI speaks a lot and always dresses like he's going for a wedding, but he is a very good marksman and on his day, I would find it difficult to beat him. He is very vain though, and stuck in his ways. I've always told him to realign his quivers or to at least give my three-arrow system a try. He never listens.

These are just tools, son. I don't use the three-arrow system all the time. I didn't even need to use it to cut down Grandsire but it's just a useful thing to know. It makes your bowmanship more efficient at times, especially when you're dealing with a mass of enemies. Wisdom never goes waste, but who's to tell him?

So as you can see, he's getting tired. The arrogance that formerly shone on his face has now become entrenched in lines that criss-cross it. This is not a man looking for glory; it's a man fighting for his life. It is a good thing our contingent is at hand to rescue him. Krishna directs some warriors to go and intercept Ashwatthama, Sushasana, Kripa and Bhurisravas.

Bhurisravas breaks through with some of those ghastly white soldiers they sent to kill me yesterday. Satyaki takes them down, a fraction slower than he normally would. Bhurisravas is fresh and he is, as Satyaki would say, 'a fighting man'. His arrow cuts through Satyaki's bow and another one knocks him on the helmet.

There is history here, son. One of those little founts of family gossip that keep conversations with distant relatives from meandering into silence.

Bhurisravas's father Somadatta was defeated in a wrestling match for the hand of a Yadava noblewoman by Satyaki's father, Sini, who was the champion of Vasudeva, a Yadava nobleman. You see, Vasudeva was a better statesman than a warrior and found it was better to have a warrior of Sini's calibre to fight on his behalf. A wise decision. The woman in question was Devaki, Krishna's mother. Without Sini, Krishna would not have been born. The families have been feuding ever since. When Satyaki learned Bhurisravas was taking his Yadavas to Suyodhana's faction, he immediately signed up for ours. I suspect, if Bhurisravas was fighting for us, we would see him on the other end of the battlefield.

Why there needs to be a competition to gain the favour of a woman is something I've never understood. How is being the best wrestler in a pit enough indication that the man will be a good husband?

Now, the bards make up all kinds of strange stories about what happened with your aunt, Draupadi. I've heard one where I shot the eye of a fish from its reflection in the water and saved Draupadi from the clutches of Suyodhana. There's even one where she rejects Radheya because of his *suta* upbringing. All these stories deliberately came up before the war to rally more people to our cause. The truth of the matter, you should know, is Drupada had already spoken to Mother about marrying her off to all of us. If a man can have many wives, why can't a woman have many husbands—that was his rationale. Also, the kind of lives we lead, if one brother died, there would be others to keep her married for the rest of her life. We married Draupadi because we needed allies. Over the years, our mutual regard for one another turned to love.

Coming back to Satyaki.

He's kneeling on his chariot floor with two arrows in his chest. Bhurisravas comes on foot from behind and swats his helmet off his head, dragging him out by his hair. He has a sword in his hand. Will he have his revenge?

'Arjuna, Bhurisravas,' says Krishna from his seat.

Revenge isn't destined for Bhurisravas in this life. I fix an arrow and take aim at his sword. It is a crescent-headed arrow. I drag the bowstring behind my ear. Shot with enough force, the arrow can split his sword in two. I release the string.

The arrow misses.

It hits Bhurisravas's wrist that does not have any protection and cuts it off. The sword, still clutched in his hand, spins and falls next to him. Bhurisravas looks at the bleeding stump of his hand and tries to understand what is happening.

'You!' he screams, more in pain than rage.

Krishna stands up and speaks loudly for our troops to hear. 'The murderers of Abhimanyu do not deserve a fair fight.'

The conches of the Indraprastha contingent begin to blow on his command. The Kaurava troops are stunned. For the first time since yesterday, I realize you're not with us, son.

The conches and Bhurisravas's stump reminds me. The blood colouring the ground, the wind laden with the smell of the dead, Krishna's dark limbs dancing in the air—it's all too much.

I see Satyaki pick up the sword with the hand still grasping it; he uses it to hack Bhurisravas's neck. It's not a clean strike. Three chops and the head dangles off the neck with a thread of skin. The fourth one beheads him.

'Beheaded by his own hand. This is surely suicide!' I hear him scream, dangling the sword with the hand at the enemy. The Kauravas are enraged. They try to get him but our chariots surround Satyaki and he is lost in the madness.

Where are you, son?

I lost you in the battlefield yesterday. You're not here but I don't feel like I've lost you. I feel your presence here, watching me, on the chariot. Not hovering above me like a spirit, but here, standing next to me. There's no flesh but I can feel you. No voice, but I know you're listening. Krishna says you were murdered yesterday. Then why do I feel you here?

He takes the chariot further inside. Bhima and Satyaki are standing on the ones next to me. My arms are working on their own volition. Like machines. I don't know who is controlling them. I see arrows getting released and people falling. When I see an arrow, my legs move. Bhurisravas's chariot lies empty behind us. His banner with the wooden tent stake limps over the wooden flagpole, almost covering its shame. Ashwatthama's lion tail banner comes into view and then moves away. Krishna is talking—a steady stream of words—not the mighty river that Satyaki utters or the trickle that emerges from Dhristadyumna.

It is growing dark, son.

They say after death, the human spirit—the aatman—stays around its loved ones for thirteen days till its release from the earthly planes. I never really believed that and yet you're with me here. You must be.

The sky is losing colour quickly. Faster than normal. The troops around us stop fighting to look at the colour being drained from the sky. They are getting frightened.

'The sun is breaking,' I hear Krishna say.

I look around even as the fighting around me ceases. Is the sun really breaking? I'm tempted to sneak a glance at it when I hear Krishna roar at the troops.

'No one looks at the sun! No one!'

Everyone looks down except me. I glance at Krishna who is looking at something.

Taken aback, he points, 'There, Arjuna! Jayadratha. Kill him now.'

I see a man in grey armour looking as bewildered as the rest of us. His bow is to his side. He has a familiar face. I've fought him before. But he could be out of range. I take out an arrow, fix it on my bow and pull the string back as far as I possibly can. I hear Shakuni call out.

'The day has ended. Stop fighting!'

Krishna screams, his throat hoarse with the effort.

'No one look at the sun!'

The last sliver of daylight is gulped by darkness; I release the arrow and then another one in quick succession. The entire battlefield is submerged in darkness. The troops begin to panic. They clatter against each other, the horses neigh wildly, and the elephants—few as they are—trumpet loudly. Voices everywhere illuminate the darkness that is now invading our heads.

'Leave the field!'

'The end has come!'

'Keep calm!'

And through it all, there's Krishna's voice.

'Don't look at the sun!'

A few moments later, the sky becomes purple and the darkness begins to fade. The sun peaks through; it pushes out of the womb of darkness and cries forth with its light. The sun is reborn. So are the soldiers. They stand as if in a daze. No one fights. Everyone just stands on their spots, trying to comprehend what just happened. Krishna's voice is heard. He stands on one of the horses and his voice carries through the silence.

'The sun sees the injustice to Pandavas and helps them take revenge on Jayadratha, murderer of Abhimanyu. The vow is complete! Arjuna's oath to kill the murderer today is accomplished. The Gods are with us!'

He waves his hand and, as if on cue, the conches boom.

RADHEYA

WHAT OATH? WHAT VOW?

I saw Jayadratha's neck being hit by an arrow with great force as the sun disappeared, or broke, as I heard someone say. The arrow was followed by another, and the next thing I knew, Jayadratha's head had been cleanly lifted off his body and was lost between the chariot wheels.

Before I could take all this in, Krishna began to speak about a fulfilled oath and the Pandava conches began blaring. That was when their troops began to charge. Krishna started shouting louder, 'Even the Lord averted his eyes from our revenge. God fights with the Pandavas.' Our troops began to panic as the Pandavas cut into them. There was danger here. If the Pandavas could get behind the reserve, they could attack us from the back and cause even more damage. We had to stop them from pushing through.

Nothing had happened to the sun. I had heard of this phenomenon before. An astronomer in Anga once told me how every hundred or so years, the sun would be swallowed and spit out by the darkness. It was a scientific phenomenon just like sunrise and sunset. Nothing more, nothing less. I saw the sun disappear and knew it would reappear, unlike the troops who thought it had gone for good. And now, they believed Krishna when he said it was God's rage and he was God's avenging hand. Something had to be done. The phenomenon was about as divine as my arse was hairless. I began shouting.

'It's not divine! He's lying!'

But the troops didn't listen and jostled to get out of the way of the Pandavas who were making easy work of them. I saw Kripa and Ashwatthama attack Arjuna, who held them both off. An arrow bounced off my chariot. I wondered whether saying it was a scientific phenomenon would mean anything to these men consumed by their own fear. It definitely did not have the same ring as 'God's rage'. An arrow hit me and went deep in my arm. I shouted in pain and looked out to see Satyaki wiping his forehead and fitting another arrow. I wrenched out the arrow from my arm and fitted one of my own as another arrow came towards me. I ducked as it flew over my head and aimed a shot at Satyaki's middle. It went straight and punched him through the gut. I saw him fall. Hopefully, he was dead.

My chariot pushed through the surge of troops that were trying to head away from the Pandavas. I saw Arjuna in front. There was only one way to end the panic.

YUDHISHTHIRA

I AWOKE WITH a sense that I had experienced this before: The feeling of lying on a chariot floor, helpless, and knowing that something awful had happened without knowing what it was.

Abhimanyu.

My brothers.

Prativindhya.

I got up with a start. The chariot was still.

'What has happened, charioteer?' I asked, dreading the answer.

He turned around. Sahadeva's charioteer was still with me.

'You fell unconscious before the charge. I took you back on Lord Dhristadyumna's order. He's told me not to go anywhere without his permission.'

I seemed to be spending a major chunk of the war unconscious. I cursed myself for being weak.

'Move towards the fight,' I said, waving weakly with my hand.

'Apologies, my lord, Lord Dhristadyumna commanded me to stay here with you. He said we can't lose you.'

'It's nearly night-time. Hasn't the fighting stopped?'

He shrugged. 'The sun is disappearing.'

I saw the darkness spreading across the sky and averted my gaze. I had heard an eclipse could make one blind.

'What a time for this to happen,' I muttered to myself.

'Is this the end of the world?' asked the charioteer. His voice quavered a little.

'No, not if you take me to the front now.'

'I'm sorry, my lord. Lord Dhristadyumna…'

'Do you want the world to end?' I interrupted.

'I don't believe your going to the front line will change that, my lord.'

I sighed. Where did Sahadeva get this one from?

'Okay, the world isn't ending but I have to see Dhristadyumna. Could you please take me to him? I want to check if my brothers are all right.'

He was silent for a moment, and then, he led the chariot ahead. As the darkness fell, our troops were still. I could feel the fear rise from them like stench.

'It's all right. It's natural. It's just the sun healing itself. It will be back, I promise. No one look at the sun until it does,' I shouted, and repeated it to try and quell the panic.

We reached Dhristadyumna who was trying to calm his troops the same way. A few moments later, the sky changed colour and the sun began to reveal itself. The troops in the front line from both factions saw everyone in the light of a new sun and began to regard each other a little awkwardly, not sure whether to fight or not. The sun had disappeared and taken all the aggression with it. For a brief moment, I allowed myself to wonder if this meant peace.

The next moment, my musing was shattered. I saw Drona

burst forth with a host of chariots, scattering arrows like petals. Dhristadyumna saw me, but looked through me as he turned his chariot around and headed towards Drona with his father Drupada close at his heels.

I hadn't fought at all today. I gripped a javelin, determined to make one kill at least, and felt ashamed of myself the next moment for wanting to deprive someone of their life just to save face with my brothers and fellow warriors. Enough lives had been lost. Another epiphany bubbled up; we couldn't win this war unless everyone on the other side was dead. Or at least their commanders. I saw Drona's chariot make its way through the field and felt an intense hatred for him at that moment. This war would end with his death.

RADHEYA

THE SUN WAS actually setting this time. Not like the last deception. And yet the Pandavas were showing no signs of stopping, neither were our boys. I think we all feared it was going to happen again and did not want to be caught unawares. The light was fading fast, so I took out a torch I kept in my chariot, soaked its head with oil and lit it. I was immediately greeted by a flurry of arrows.

A few torches came up on other chariots as troops huddled together next to them. A few troops began shouting out their regiment names or their tribes and were immediately cut down if they were close to an enemy. Like blind men, we stalked the field slowly and cautiously. None of the chariots charged and every man on the field, be it on horse, elephant or foot, sought security in the stillness and quiet. The field soon became silent as no one wanted to present themselves as a target. Sound had become sight and the slightest noise could lead to death.

The light on our chariots did little except present us as targets, but since the light did not illuminate our battle standards and presented our faces more in shadows, no one wanted to take the chance of killing an ally. At the same time, since there was no official recognition of the day's end, we all moved around slowly hoping someone would put an end to the day's fighting.

The end of the day was normally announced with a slew of conch blasts and drumbeats that rose to a crescendo. An official chronicler of the war from both ends would wait until the light escaped our vision and killing became more difficult than usual. At the beginning of the war, our chronicler, in a fit of enthusiasm, would deliberately wait several moments after his counterpart on the other side had blown his horn to allow our troops the excuse to kill some more. After the third day of this happening, Grandsire Bhishma summoned the chronicler and had him executed on the spot. The new one had specific instructions to begin the blowing of the conches before or with the Pandava faction, otherwise his head would join his predecessor in the dead pit—as an evening snack for the dogs.

Needless to say, we had been very prompt in exiting the battlefield since then. Today, it looked like the chroniclers themselves were confused.

It was a cold, windless night. My chariot moved slowly into the darkness. The men around me, illuminated weakly by the orange flame, looked like ghosts in the river of the dead. More chariots began to get illuminated and a few foot soldiers even began carrying torches. From where they got these, I don't know. Maybe the chariots had spares too. I heard a voice break the silence nearby. It sounded like Bhima.

I whispered to my charioteer to take us towards the sound. In the faint torch light, I saw Bhima. He had his hands wrapped around Suyodhana's brother Sukarna's neck, choking the life out of him. I quickly lifted my bow and nocked an arrow but he walked out of the firelight. I threw down my bow, lifted a sword and the torch, and ran towards where I had seen them last. Sukarna's body was a few steps away. His eyes were open wide in fear, his body was still. Another brother of Suyodhana dead.

I looked around and saw the frightened faces of soldiers in the dark. I couldn't make out if they were from our side or not, so I got back on my chariot, mounted the torch and peered out to see if I could recognize anyone within its narrow circle of light.

A horse neighed next to me; I turned around, clutching my sword tightly. A chariot came into view, then another. Ashwatthama and Kripa. They had lit torches on their chariots too, resulting in a little field of light. Some soldiers, recognizing us, moved towards us like moths.

'*Suta*, you could have saved Jayadratha.'

For a moment, I didn't realize Kripa was talking to me. I looked past Ashwatthama to see him. I couldn't make out his face but his body was turned in my direction. It was silent in our part of the battlefield. All the soldiers heard it.

'Kripacharya...,' said Ashwatthama with gentle disapproval.

I couldn't count how many brothers of Suyodhana had died today and this man was worried about some idiot king of Sindhu?

'Kripa,' I said, 'I have no faith in your theories. If they were any good, we would have won the war by now. As it happens, we must pull your dead weight.'

I heard the rasp of a sword being drawn out its scabbard.

'The only dead weight here will be yours.'

Ashwatthama shouted at us with some urgency.

'Kripacharya, Radheya! Fighting has begun.'

He was right. More chariots had joined our immediate

perimeter. We had become a small honeycomb of light and were now recognizable as a Kaurava unit. A cluster of lit chariots approached us and a few arrows with fire heads flew in our direction.

GHATOTKACHA

Everyone around me was lighting torches. I had seen the men light them on our way back to camp every day after the battle. They were small, no longer than the distance between the tip of my finger and my elbow—like a flower with a thick stalk and a large head whose petals faced the sky. The centre of the torch sat on an oily mess of rope which on being burned by the sparks of flint stones became a fat ball of fire that could last an hour or more, depending on the wind.

I never cared for the light.

Sight can be a poor ally in the jungle. Rain, smoke, leaves, and so many other things disrupt it. On the other hand, darkness is natural. Light is often the intruder and gets snuffed out just as easily as it comes. In the jungle, we've long been taught not to trust our eyes, but our nose, ears and the sensation of touch. Sight brings false security. And the lack of it brings fear.

On the battlefield too, men were stumbling onto one another, despite the firelight. It was not adequate. It could never be. Sooner or later, the darkness would swallow it.

I could smell, almost taste the fear in the air. It cut through the scent of rotting flesh and fire. I brought out my hatchet now.

Kauravas were in front. I knew this because I could hear them whispering amongst themselves, wondering where the Pandavas were. My brothers and I stalked their ragged formation. Within a few moments, their bodies were lying on the ground, noiseless in death as they never were in life.

The brothers and I were happiest in the shadows. We dispersed in different directions. No order was given, or taken. The night had different rules from the day. If the mob held sway in the day, the king of the night held court alone. I stalked a company of twelve Kaurava soldiers and made short work of four before the rest got wind of my presence and I vanished, just as noiselessly as I arrived.

A group of chariots with lit torches were clustered in one end of the battlefield like a dim sun in the ocean of night. I sensed the men going in that direction and let them pass. I would stalk them from behind.

'You're not like the others.'

A voice snaked its way silently through the night and I sensed something move to my side and cut my arm. I crouched and held my arm that stung.

'Are you like me?'

The voice came from a different direction this time. I couldn't hear his feet. He didn't even leave a scent in his wake. He was too quick for me to touch. Seeing him was out of the question.

'Killing men in the dark is so much easier, no, little one?'

I stayed quiet, hoping his desire to talk would give me some clue of his whereabouts.

'My name is Alamvusha.'

The voice came from another direction now.

'I'm mleccha, just like you are to these people.'

I heard his steps and twisted away a moment before a sword came swinging down and hacked the ground I had stood on a moment ago. I swung my hatchet towards the side and it grazed him.

'Why are you fighting? We, the people of the hills, should not take sides with those of the plains.'

'I'm not from a hill,' I replied to coax his position.

'Then where are you from, little one?'

The 'little one' bit was obviously a ploy to guide my imagination towards stretching his proportions. I had struck him. He was no bigger than me.

'Come close so I can tell you.'

He chuckled. 'Maybe when this is over.'

Another swing of the sword. This time, I heard the blade cut through the air. I turned and aimed a blow at where I thought he was standing. My hatchet connected again. With flesh this time, not mere skin. To his credit, he didn't cry out. I had hit him on the calf. The right one perhaps.

His voice was strained this time. 'Why are you fighting? Leave your weapon and walk away. I'm done toying with you.'

I stayed silent.

'Little one, this will not end well. Leave.'

I took a silent breath. He spoke again after a few moments.

'Very well, then. I'm leaving. You're spared, little one.'

I didn't hear anything for a few moments. I couldn't sense his presence either. Suddenly, I heard footsteps—one slower than the other. I heard the swish of a sword at me. I twisted, but it cut my side and got stuck in my ribs for a moment before he pulled it out. I caught his sword arm and hacked it hard with my hatchet. The sword fell and he twisted out of my grasp, but not quickly enough. I aimed another blow, this time across his head, and he stumbled senseless for a moment. I grabbed his neck and with my other hand, wrenched off his helmet and smashed his face hard against my knee. He had long hair and I held it tight as I struck his neck with my hatchet. Once, twice, and then two times more, till I tore his head from his body. I could feel the blood sluicing through the stump of his neck—warm, like a hot water spring. He was not so big. A little shorter than I was—now without a head.

It was now that the blow across my ribs called out. It stung terribly. I crumpled on the ground and gasped. The pain began to subside, slowly turning into a deep throbbing that seemed to vibrate inside my ribs. I blinked. My vision was blurry, or was it the night? It had been a long day. Maybe it was the fatigue. I stood up slowly. A ringing sound seemed to chime in my ear. My head felt heavy and began to spin. I collapsed to my knees and shook my head vigorously, trying to push away the curtain of heaviness that threatened to distort my perceptions. The blood flowed freely from my side and I couldn't seem to staunch it.

I held Alamvusha's hair and twisted it into a knot, dragging the head on the mud with me.

I didn't know why I did this.

I was not angry with him. Not particularly. War had no rules. Abhimanyu came to my mind—the only one of my cousins I had known at all. I had met them all before the battle. Prativindhya, Somadatta, and the rest of them—names I couldn't even remember.

The whole camp had been outraged yesterday, at the manner

he had died. It was not honourable, they had said. I kept my counsel but I wondered what made it less honourable. The fact that he had been killed because we couldn't breach their formation or the fact that he had willingly put his life at risk by venturing into the *chakravyuha* alone? He knew what he was getting into, or should have at least, when the war began.

And so did I.

I couldn't feel my limbs until I really squeezed my muscles. But I knew I was still the master of them. My nose was blocked and I could smell the iron scent of blood filling it. I walked, dragging Alamvusha's head back towards the centre of the battlefield where all the torches seemed to be clustered. A lot of other soldiers did the same. None of them noticed I was walking around with the head of a man—like an animal on a leash. If they did, they thought nothing of it. Outside the perimeter of light, there was little fighting. Where the light began, the death began too.

Maybe the world was better in darkness.

I stumbled into the fighting. I felt chariots rumble close by and followed their path. No one attacked me. This was the Pandava side of the battlefield. I was confident.

I looked down and Alamvusha's head stared back at me. I looked at my enemy for the first time in the dim light of the torches that surrounded us. His eyes were wide open, his mouth showing all his teeth.

'Ghatotkacha! Ghatotkacha! You're wounded.'

A woman's voice. It was either Shikhandi or I was hallucinating. I turned in that direction and tried to say something, but no voice left my throat. A parched rattling sound emanated from it instead. My tongue was numb. Likely dead. I turned away and walked quickly towards another chariot. I could hear her voice calling from behind, but it was soon lost. The ringing in my ear was growing louder.

'Ghatotkacha!' A smooth voice this time—a man's.

'Radheya's up front. Go with these troops and stop him. We need to head towards the rear. Drona's breaking our back.'

It sounded like Uncle Krishna. I heard Shikhandi's voice call out once again. This time, it was closer. I walked away, clenching my hatchet tightly. The doors of my senses closed one by one. I looked in front and saw Radheya a few steps away, surrounded by a curtain of light and some foot soldiers. My mind travelled a little. I never thought I would die like this on a battlefield. Somehow, I always saw myself in the forest when the time came to take my leap, surrounded by my wife and grown-up children. I wondered if Appa would be proud of me. Was Arjuna proud of Abhimanyu?

I lifted my arm and swung Alamvusha's head around in circles before throwing it into the Kaurava line. A howl of outrage greeted this act as they drew away. I took out my stabbing spear and began swinging wildly, creating more space between us. A spear lunged at me and I heard it tear through the silence of the air, only for a moment before it stabbed me. The ringing in my head was louder. My eyes were nearly empty of sight now, and my nose could detect the scent of death.

I saw the man that Uncle Krishna was talking about on his chariot, a few feet away from me. The man he called Radheya. A great sadness overwhelmed me as I realized I wouldn't be able to take Appa back to the forest. Back to Amma, to end her loneliness. I looked at Radheya once more. He was shouting orders and had his bow drawn. I waited for him to turn away.

I was ready to take the great leap. I clenched my weapons tightly, closed my eyes and leaped in the direction of his voice that drew me towards it like a noose.

SUSHASANA

THE SUN DISAPPEARED and then reappeared a few moments later. And then we were plunged into darkness again. What was happening? The troops around me began to panic and I heard one of them shout that God had abandoned the Kurus. My feet began to tremble but I took a deep breath and recited the phrase that Father taught me to repeat to myself whenever I was frightened. It was probably one of the very few things he ever taught me.

'Sushasana, there is probably a good explanation for all this.'

I repeated it to myself over and over again but it didn't have its general calming effect on me. I looked around and recognized Suyodhana's face, lit by a torch a little distance away. He would know what to do. He always did.

Once, when I was a child, one of the nurses in the palace told me a story about ghosts eating young boys while they slept. She added for her own wicked mirth that there were ghosts like that in the Hastinapura palace too. The bitch was probably trying to have some fun with me. Anyway, I could not sleep from that night onwards. I lagged behind in the Gurukul and lived in mortal fear of ghosts. One day, Father came to inspect our progress at the training ground and I burst into tears and told him everything. He laughed and told me there was nothing to be afraid of. He said there were no such things as ghosts, and then, he shared this phrase—or mantra as he called it—to repeat the next time someone told me such a fanciful story.

So I repeated the mantra to myself over and over again, hoping it would protect me from the ghosts. All the other boys in the Gurukul laughed, including some of my own half-brothers. The only one who didn't was Suyodhana. When I would lie wet with sweat and the shame of my bowels, he would come silently and lie in the bed with me, with his arm around me. He did it every night for eighteen days, till finally on the nineteenth, exhaustion overcame me and I fell asleep. The night after, I went to sleep on my own and he never came again. I had beaten the fear. He never brought it up again. Not even as a dirty weapon in an argument.

His mother—and Father's first wife Gandhari—was sick most of the time, and would rarely come out. Father's own dalliances were well-known in the palace and there were many stories about how she had tied a piece of silk cloth around her eyes to blind herself to my father's numerous affairs with the palace wenches and any other woman he could find. We grew up in a palace full of bastards and all of us spent our time trying to get Father's eye, blind as it was.

It was evident to most of us that Suyodhana would be king one day because he was the eldest son of Father's first wife. But Father never made us feel as if we were simply an inconvenient byproduct of his lust. And if there was one thing I could give him credit for, it was the fact that he brought up all of us as if we were princes. Perhaps, the rationale behind this was to put as many heads as possible on the succession line between him and Pandu.

So, when the Pandavas came into our lives unannounced and rudely staked their claim to the throne, we all rebelled. And apart from Yuyutsu, who always felt he could have been king and never liked Suyodhana anyway, all of us rallied behind Suyodhana who was the eldest of the half-brothers and could be counted on to take care of us unlike the Pandavas who would have probably driven us out of the palace.

My mind wandered back to the battlefield. My chariot reached Suyodhana who was talking to Shakuni. It seemed more like he was ranting.

'Guruji is the only one who can save this from becoming a complete rout. Get him now!'

'Leave him, Suyodhana. Let him perish, he went ahead because of his own folly. Let us go behind together.'

'Now!' I heard Suyodhana say.

Shakuni barked some order and his Gandhara cavalry formed around him, galloping ahead. I went up to Suyodhana to make sense of what was happening.

'Is it true? Have the Gods abandoned us?'

'Makes no difference. We will win this war without them,' he said as if it was the most ordinary thing on earth. His confidence gave me courage.

'Tell me then, what must I do?'

'Follow Shakuni. Get Guruji out of the front and back among us. We can't lose him.'

I thought I heard fear in his voice for the first time that day. He didn't care about breaking through the Pandava line, he just wanted Guruji back. I assembled a ragtag bunch of chariots around me and we followed Shakuni into the Pandava centre. We didn't have to plunge too deep though. Most of the Pandavas were scattered and were trying to head back and reform.

Guruji was not very far ahead and I saw Shakuni reach him without any trouble. He began talking to Drona who threw his bow down on the chariot floor in disgust as his chariot turned around and retreated.

Kritavarma and his Narayanis formed up swiftly and followed him. Shakuni and his Gandhara cavalry came at the very end. There would be no further assault today. We turned around too, and I headed towards Suyodhana, hoping to be the first to tell him the good news that Guruji was alive.

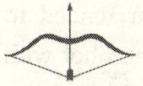

RADHEYA

A DARK AND bald warrior holding a hatchet and a spear took a step and leaped over a line of infantry towards me. Luckily, I had an arrow fixed and shot it square in his chest before I jumped out of my chariot. The arrow smashed into his heart. He wasn't wearing armour so he was probably dead before he fell on my chariot floor.

A great howl was heard from the front. A few more like him, dark and dressed in tribal costumes, pushed through their own troops up front. He must have been a tribal chief or something. I lifted his body and my soldiers put it on the ground. We backed away as the tribals came snarling at us. Once they retrieved the body, they disappeared into the Pandava line.

Rowdy tribals. Always difficult to deal with. They were hired more as arrow fodder than anything else. They were cheap and would run at anything if drunk enough. I had little time to waste on a tribal chief.

Narasimha and I somehow managed to get our Angas in some fighting shape. We were holding back the Pandava advance almost single-handedly as most of the army scattered once the night fighting began.

I was down to my irons now. A quiver of a hundred iron-headed arrows. Each of them a masterpiece. They were weighted perfectly unlike many iron arrows that tended to prematurely drift downwards because of the weight. Shot with enough strength, one could probably cut through an elephant. It was going to be impossible to retrieve them tonight. Each arrow used would be one lost. I looked at Narasimha who was shooting arrow after arrow into a mass of soldiers.

'Narasimha, I'm down to my irons. Could you lend me a quiver of bronze arrows?'

'Can't do, m'lord. If I were to lend you a quiver, I'd be closer to using my irons. The King of Anga could probably afford another quiver of iron arrows. A humble soldier such as myself is not so economically advantaged.'

I cursed Narasimha for being a stingy son of a bitch and picked out another iron arrow.

The twins Nakula and Sahadeva were ahead and more fitting targets for my iron warheads. I took aim in the dim light and sent an arrow that hit Sahadeva full in his chest. It wasn't a particularly clean strike as he was wearing mail over his breastplate, but it probably cracked through the mail and metal breastplate, and broke his skin at the very least. He fell down on his knees, winded, and his twin Nakula, who was close by as always, took him out of his chariot before I could finish his life.

Without the twins, the Pandavas in the van had no leaders. Sensing the shift, my Angas pushed through and broke their formation, sending them into retreat. I told my charioteer to take us closer to them. I would stalk and kill the pair together. I nocked an arrow as my chariot approached their retreating line.

A conch sounded in the *rishabh* note, then another, until a series of horns went up and cymbals began to crash together loudly. The end of the day had finally been announced.

THE FOURTEENTH NIGHT

YUDHISHTHIRA

If Dhristadyumna was to be believed, we had been on the verge of killing Drona before he had left in retreat. More credible sources, or perhaps more cynical ones, had told me that Guruji had left on his own terms, with Kritavarma comfortably pounding a hole in our centre.

Drona, his name was Drona, not Guruji, I reminded myself.

I later learned that Shikhandi had commanded the war chroniclers to announce the day's end when she saw that the war was devolving into an unruly massacre. Luckily, when the Kaurava war chroniclers heard our conches and cymbals, they promptly began sounding their own, leading to both armies leaving the field.

When the conches had sounded the day's end, it was already late evening, and by the time we trudged back wearily to camp, it was almost midnight. Another council would be held tomorrow morning. Shikhandi accosted me as I limped over to my tent.

'You should go and see Bhima.'

'What happened?'

'Ghatotkacha. I was there. He died well. I'm sorry.'

Two nephews on consecutive days. It seemed like we had

been very fortunate the first twelve days. She stood with her eyes down, fixed at the mud. Abhimanyu's death had rattled her. She was fond of the boy as we all were. None of us had really known Ghatotkacha before the war.

My thoughts returned to Prativindhya, who I had known all my life either through letters or occasional visits, who was my blood, and that of a recognizable world, unlike Ghatotkacha whose world began and ended in the forest. I felt ashamed of myself momentarily and walked away from Shikhandi, towards Bhima's tent. He wasn't there.

I checked in Arjuna's, but couldn't find him there either. Arjuna was sitting silently on his bed. I decided not to bother him and went to the other tents. Sahadeva had been injured and was sleeping, his tent heavy with the scent of oil and herbs. Nakula's tent was empty. His retainer told me he had gone to the stables. I didn't know whether they had heard about what had happened.

I began to panic. Would Bhima do something foolish like take his own life? Or worse, had he gone seeking revenge in the Kaurava camp? An idea struck me and I walked quickly down to the enclosure of Ghatotkacha's tribe. The enclosure was silent tonight. No singing or humming. I walked inside and saw the tribals gathered together, surrounding something. I pushed my way through the crowd to the centre and saw Bhima.

He cradled Ghatotkacha's dead body on a bier made of wood as a couple of men stood behind him, waiting for him to leave so they could wash it. He saw me and left the body. He fell on me and started crying.

'He shouldn't have gone. Abhimanyu and him should have stayed back with the other sons,' he sobbed loudly.

'Bhima...Bhima...,' I could only say his name to try and soothe him. I had nothing left. No words. No wisdom. For a moment my heart went out to the Kauravas who had to see their brothers butchered every day before their eyes. Who offered them comfort?

I pulled Bhima away as the tribe conducted their funeral rites. I led him to his tent and told his retainers to put him in bed, preferably after drugging him. They nodded and led him inside.

Arjuna had become a walking ghost. A hollow husk of a human being whose only contact seemed to be with the imaginary spirit of his son. Was Bhima going to become the same? If Prativindhya was indeed dead, what would become of me?

I hurried to Prativindhya's tent, hoping to find him there. The tent was empty.

THE FIFTEENTH DAY

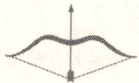

RADHEYA

I'M NOT SURE I got any sleep at all. The night, or what was left of it when we got back, seemed to have ended before it began. The cocks began slaughtering the silence of the morning almost as soon as I got into bed. I somehow got my hand on a jug of cold water and doused it over my head to wake up. The cold water stitched my senses together instantly and I gasped loudly, more to get my retainer's attention than anything else.

He came running and the concern on his face deflated into relief. 'Thank god, sire! I thought your wounds were acting up.'

I grunted and shook my head vigorously. A brass tumbler of hot milk and honey later, every notion of sleep was banished from the kingdom of my being.

There was no reason to be cheerful today. Jayadratha was dead, the army had been in another embarrassing rout. Our morale had probably found a place in the underworld. There was still no sign of Yudhishthira among us.

And yet, I felt light as a cloud. Perhaps I was getting used to failure.

I asked my retainer to summon Shatrujeet and Varahamira. They came almost instantly—Varahamira and most of Shatrujeet, whose head was tied in a bandage and smelled obnoxious. The bandage circled his entire head like a turban, covering his forehead and eyebrows, along with his entire scalp.

I was glad to see both of them alive. The only spies I could trust in this camp.

'So you've covered yourself in glory, have you, Shatrujeet? How did you manage to lose only half of your head?'

Shatrujeet grinned.

'Mace, m'lord. Someone made a point of introducing it to the side of my head. Cracked through my helmet. We call it a Magadha kiss from where I come, Magadha being famous for its maces and all that.'

I smiled. 'And what is Anga famous for, my brave?'

'Why, your lordship, of course. The King of Anga. Finest in all realms. Not a soul like him.'

Varahamira had apparently had enough and interrupted our little banter.

'My lord, there is an urgent matter that requires your immediate attention.'

I nodded.

He began, almost relishing the moroseness of his news, 'The troops, my lord, are losing faith in the cause. News of Arjuna's vow has spread.'

'What vow? There was no vow. No one knew of anything till Krishna conveniently announced it.'

'We're not sure of that, my lord. Some troops claim that he made the vow in front of them in the dying moments of the thirteenth day.'

'Nonsense, he probably didn't even know about Abhimanyu's death then. And why kill Jayadratha? He had the least to do with the entire thing. Drona, Sushasana's son and I are more responsible, no?'

I had bullied Varahamira into silence. Shatrujeet spoke.

'What my friend and esteemed colleague is trying to say is that soldiers' minds are strange places. They make up truths every moment. Churn them out relentlessly. That's their job, so that they don't distract the hands from the real work. Sometimes, the truth may not be real, but in the soldier's mind, it's as clear and pure as the Ganga.'

'Stop speaking in riddles, man.'

'It may not be real but it is true for the soldiers, and that's all that matters.'

He was right. Something had to be done, and fast.

'Plus, after yesterday's sun-disappearing trick, the soldiers are wondering if Krishna did it so that Arjuna could take his revenge.'

I sighed, 'It's nature's way of renewing the sun. There's nothing out of the ordinary about it.'

'Perhaps, my lord. But at that precise moment before nightfall? And to help Arjuna complete his vow?'

'There was no vow!' I snapped. It was like banging one's head against a wall. Nothing could be gained from this. If Shatrujeet and Varahamira, experienced campaigners as they were, were not fully convinced, then I could only imagine the rest of the troops.

I dismissed them and got ready. I wanted a clean face today. My retainer took out a razor and applied an ointment that softened the stubble on my skin emerging confidently since I joined the war. He ran the razor over my face, across my cheeks and neck, gliding it gently over the skin. I looked into the mirror and observed his progress.

The mirror began to blur slightly. I blinked and all the edges fell back into place. Maybe it was all the stress. A towel soaked in hot water was run over my face and I was ready to face the day—and stare it down till it cowered and vanished into dusk.

My retainer had my breastplate ready. I was feeling a little sore from yesterday so I asked him to give me a lighter leather one, with chain mail draped over it. He looked surprised. I looked at him coldly and made the request again, which is when he complied.

My retainers, spies, generals—they all felt they could express themselves in front of me freely. Happiness, surprise, resentment, fear—every emotion was at their disposal to pick and throw at me unlike the staff of the other princes who were forbidden to display any emotion when asked to do a task. Maybe it was because my staff thought I was really like them and not like the other princes. I didn't know if it was a good thing. I found myself wishing for people from my retinue to actually do what I told them without looking surprised, worried, or like Narasimha yesterday, refusing outright.

But the thought soon extinguished itself. The new armour was light and I rolled my arms around, delighted at the new mobility it offered me. Now I only had to make sure I did not get into any sword or mace fights, and that not too many iron arrows pierced me on the field today.

A group of kings, already armoured, nodded as I walked past them into the council tent. It would be a short meeting today. The time for battle was almost upon us. I saw Drona pick up the Speaking Staff and usher everyone in. Sanjaya Gavalgani stood next to him with Suyodhana, who was glaring at the ground.

'Hurry up, haven't got time,' growled Drona as everyone quickened their paces. I stood in a corner; Shakuni came and stood next to me. I looked at him and smiled, he did the same. He looked in Drona's direction and sighed. Then, he spoke in his soft, cultured tone.

'I heard Kripa got on your nerves yesterday. I fully sympathize. He lives off Drona's brilliance which is somewhat fading.'

I looked at him. I always knew Shakuni disliked Drona, but to say it openly like this was not his style. Kripa was Drona's brother-in-law, and chief of staff—his Narasimha.

'This army needs a new leader. In spirit, if not in actual title.'

Drona interrupted our conversation.

'Yesterday night saw some of our allies leave without warning. Once the war is won, they will be dealt with harshly. And it will be won soon. Yesterday was a success. Sanjaya, tell us our numbers.'

Sanjaya had never been a favourite of Grandsire and Drona, in all his four days of being in charge, hadn't even cared to acknowledge him until yesterday.

'Two hundred and fifty chariots. Thirty-six elephants. Four thousand, eight hundred and fifty-two men killed. Forty-six maimed and unavailable for duty again. Twenty-two men have been seriously injured but can return if the war resumes tomorrow. On an average, yesterday's formation was a successful one. Losses, despite the night's panic, were less than three-fourth of the thirteenth day.'

I will never know what pleasure Sanjaya got from rattling off these numbers. All the kings were mighty impressed though, as people mostly are when they come across numbers as a tool of expression. I suspect that is why Grandsire Bhishma had him tag along. The numbers were smoke and mirrors in Drona's and my opinion. They gave a sense of brick and mortar when there was nothing but sand that could quickly vanish between our fingers. Our army was bigger and our losses may have been smaller but that could alone not determine if we were in a position to win the battle today.

Sanjaya continued rattling off figures and the eyes of the other allies glazed over, content. The fools did not want to analyse what he was saying. For them, the fact that our losses had been less was enough to indicate that yesterday was a success. Did they even know what the troops were thinking?

Shakuni continued, 'This army is not going to last very long at this rate. I'm sure your spies have told you about the unrest among the soldiery?'

Trust Shakuni to know everything. Shatrujeet and Varahamira had not been careful in covering their tracks.

'*That* is the heart of the army, not these sheep here lulled by Sanjaya's little numbers. The troops need a leader of flesh and blood, not the grey hair they've been accustomed to for the past fourteen days.'

Sanjaya paused and Shakuni looked at me for the first time in our conversation.

'I have enough at stake when it comes to Suyodhana, as you probably know. He's not only a dear nephew but also a generous ally. He will give me control over the northern iron mines of the Panchalas if we win, and some Yadava territory if we're able to trounce them spectacularly. This is all I have left. My sons Vrisha and Achala have been taken in the war. All the iron in the world cannot take their place. But something needs to.

I need to get something out of this battle, do you understand?'

There was, for a fleeting moment, desperation in his eyes—the haunted look of a man who knew he had nothing to live for but was still holding on to a thread. His eyes emptied of fear the next moment. He blinked.

'You will be our talisman. Don't do anything. Just cooperate with me. Believe me, it will all be for the best.'

Before I could protest, he exclaimed loudly in the sabha.

'The Staff, I must have the Staff! Not a word will cross the sabha till I have said my piece.'

Everyone was taken aback. Shakuni had been somewhat reticent since both his sons had died on the twelfth day. To see him in high spirits heartened everyone.

'Yesterday, Lord Radheya, here, protected our troops from being overcome after the Pandava deception.'

Jeers rang out in the sabha. Shakuni had his audience in his thrall and he strode purposefully towards the centre, claiming his stage.

'I was there. The Pandavas, drunk in the joy of their deception, were pounding our brave troops who were falling back. Radheya alone stemmed the tide and pushed back the Pandava onslaught. I was there.'

He pounded the floor with his Staff as the sabha began cheering him.

'I was there when he brought down the twins Nakula and Sahadeva, leading the van after Arjuna had retreated out of fear of the mighty lord of Anga.

'I was there, when single-handedly, he took down an entire unit of mleccha tribals, shooting an arrow straight in the heart of their chief, Ghatotkacha...'

He waited for the applause in the sabha to quieten before he delivered the next line.

'...Bhima's son...'

The sabha roared its approval.

'Jayadratha, brave Jayadratha, the king of Sindhu will be missed, but what is his sacrifice in the face of the obliteration of an entire unit of troops and the death of Bhima's son?'

'Bhima, who was humiliated yesterday by Radheya and left alone and naked without armour, who had to be borne by the Yadava brat Satyaki, away from the field. On the thirteenth day, Arjuna refused to face Radheya and lost his son. On the fourteenth, Bhima was defeated by him and ran away...and lost his son.

'The sons of Pandu are sacrificing their own children to avoid dealing with the wrath of Radheya!'

The uproar in the sabha could have probably been heard in Indraprastha.

'Arjuna has a bow, they say? Radheya does too. It's called *Vijaya*, and his iron-headed arrows are *Shakti*. *Shakti* killed the mleccha king who was terrorizing our troops. *Shakti* destroyed the rakshasa.

'I heard the Pandavas sneering yesterday that God had abandoned us. Well, it didn't look like that to me. God has delivered us Radheya who strikes fear in the hearts of their men. God has brought us Radheya who has killed their children and put an end to the Pandava line. The Pandavas hid behind a broken sun yesterday. Today, they will not be so fortunate. You say they have Arjuna? We have Radheya, and I wouldn't exchange him for the world.'

The kings were chanting my name. *My* name. Soldiers were

checking into the sabha, wondering what the commotion was all about. I looked around. Drona's face did not reveal any emotion. Suyodhana and Sushasana were beaming. Kripa was scowling and whispering to Ashwatthama in the corner. Drona walked over calmly to Shakuni and took the Staff from his hand.

'There is still a war to be won. Radheya, I hope, you will do what Bhishma and I couldn't—kill Arjuna and Bhima.' He then turned to the council and spoke, 'In the face of our reduced numbers, I believe a war of attrition is the best recourse now. We shall abandon our plan of capturing Yudhishthira. Instead, we will reduce the Pandavas, soldier by soldier, till they have no army left to fight with. Our chariot archers are going to be crucial in this phase of the plan. Today, we shall divide our army into two pincers. Suyodhana and I shall handle one. The other shall be led by Radheya and Shakuni. We shall crush the Pandavas between the two in a combined lateral movement.'

The formation was discussed in Drona's brisk style and everyone was given their positions. We walked out together—Suyodhana, Drona and I. Suyodhana was behaving like a little child.

'Get us Arjuna today, Radheya. Let's finish it.'

Drona was silent.

Suyodhana continued, 'Was that really Bhima's son? No one's heard of him. And he's a tribal too? Bhima sowed his wild oats everywhere, didn't he? Let's get you close to Arjuna today. Maybe Kritavarma can link up with your Angas. We'll give you everything you need.'

'You think it's so easy to kill Arjuna, boy?' asked Drona.

Suyodhana's face fell.

'He's my student. I know what he's capable of. Radheya

has been in battle for four days and hasn't even faced him once. Are we really pinning the hopes of the army on him?'

'Then who should we pin it on, Guruji? In four days, you've promised to deliver Yudhishthira according to some grand plan you hatched with Grandsire. Nothing has come of it. Thrice, you've been in front of the weakest of the Pandavas and have failed to dispatch him. You've fought them all—Arjuna, Bhima and the twins—yet they walk on the battlefield. Is it because you were their Guru and can't see them killed?'

Drona looked at Suyodhana. There was sadness in his eyes.

'I've grown old and weary over the course of this war. I am with you, even if you can't see that after all this while.'

He walked away slowly.

I don't suspect Suyodhana really doubted his loyalty. Drona's love for the Pandavas was a weakness and Suyodhana was just using it to make him feel guilty and perhaps fight harder.

I put on my helmet, gripped *Vijaya*, and walked to the chariot park where a diminished quiver of *Shakti* and fresh bronze heads were waiting for me.

I'd asked my staff for extra today.

YUDHISHTHIRA

I WALKED OVER TO Prativindhya's tent again in the morning and there was no sign of the boy. His tent was bare. I'd seen caves that were less desolate.

So this was how he would go. First his body, then his belongings—one by one. All that would remain would be memory. The smell of ash after the fire and smoke would depart.

Perhaps that would go too.

More practical thoughts intercepted the sadness that was threatening to overwhelm my mind. The tent was too big to haul, and hammered and staked as it was to the ground, it was more of a challenge for the average thief to steal than a sword or a writing desk or armour. I cursed myself for not being perceptive like Shikhandi and arranging for his belongings to be transported back to Indraprastha. What use was a tent to a father?

I turned around and walked away. If I stood in front of the tent any longer, my heart would break. Shikhandi saw me and guessed why I was there.

'I've still not seen his name in the lists of the dead. You must keep faith.'

Another trite remark. An uncooked line served without any

garnish of thought or emotion, delivered to fill the void within me. 'Keep faith' it seemed.

I didn't reply and walked towards the council tent. Bhima was there, whittling a piece of wood with savage intent. I sat next to him but he didn't pay attention. Arjuna was sitting still. He was not talking to himself today but his eyes had a glazed expression. Sahadeva's stomach was heavily bandaged and Nakula was sitting next to him, attentive to his every squirm. I felt quite alone at that moment.

Drupada and Virata came and sat next to me. Virata didn't look well at all and Drupada looked only mildly better. Both of them had a very rough day yesterday. Krishna walked in, followed by Dhristadyumna who began without even noticing that Chekitana hadn't arrived yet.

He arrived shortly, huffing and puffing loudly as consolation for his tardiness and stood at the entrance till the council was complete. Prativindhya couldn't have been much older than him. For a moment, I wished he was in the tent with us and Chekitana was lying somewhere in the battlefield, buried in the mud. The customary shame which always accompanied an involuntary thought did not make an appearance this time. I truly wished Chekitana was dead, and my boy alive.

I couldn't console Bhima or Arjuna either. Not that they looked like they needed it. I put my arm on Bhima who continued playing with his knife and wood that was beginning to resemble a human figure now. Was it Ghatotkacha?

'Yudhishthira?'

'Yes,' I replied without thinking.

'Will you do it?'

'Do what? Sorry you lost me there for a moment.'

'Will you, um, take the van today?'

'The van?'

'Yes, have you not followed anything we've said?'

I didn't want to admit it so I put the onus onto him.

'I was just contemplating it. Let me hear what you have in mind. Your powers of expression wane with the war.'

Dhristadyumna looked irritated but continued, 'Today's formation is a *sarvottabhadra*. A compact square. Infantry all around, and horse chariots and archers in the centre. We've lost too many soldiers. We can't afford to keep them at the back hoping for Drona to strike. At this rate, we may not have enough to fight the war so let's protect the ones we have. Instead of charging ahead for glory, let's all stay back this time.'

The remark was clearly aimed at me, along with Arjuna and Bhima who didn't look like they cared.

'Maybe we should have thought of this ten days ago instead of sending our sons to get butchered up in front,' I said, holding the anger back firmly from my voice.

Dhristadyumna looked at the floor, 'You're not the only one to lose family, Yudhishthira. If we've not been annihilated completely in the face of an overwhelming troop disadvantage, it's because of the formations I've set up.'

'I saw how successful we were on the thirteenth day.'

'Perhaps if we didn't have to use so many of our resources to protect you from Drona…'

'Perhaps if you'd actually killed him when you got the chance…'

We both glared at each other.

Virata spoke. His voice was thin, weighed down by age and war.

'I find myself echoing Krishna's sentiments from yesterday. Sometimes I don't know if our enemies are actually in this tent. You boys need to look at the matter at hand. Your own petty egos can come later. There's an army out there. Still three *akshauhini*s strong at least. We have less than half that number. Today might be the end of us all. I'm an old man. I've lived my life. I reckon Drupada here has too. The rest of you are not so fortunate and the truth is that this is a bloody mess you've gotten yourselves into. Now you can either bicker like crows until they kill you or you can try lasting another day in the hope that they won't.'

Drupada looked at him, and then at me. 'You're right about one thing, old man. This is a bloody mess we've gotten ourselves into.' He guffawed loudly, and with such glee that everyone, even Bhima, looked up at him. We hadn't heard laughter in fourteen days.

Krishna came in smoothly, 'The sons of Pandu are truly horrible people. If for nothing else, we must get them on the throne quickly as the true successors to Bhishma.'

Everyone grinned, or at least everyone except Bhima and Arjuna.

Dhristadyumna spoke now, our little argument forgotten, 'The troops are looking at you as our saviour, Arjuna. Did you really take a vow?'

Krishna spoke for him, 'What's a vow but a strong commitment to a course without deviation? What Arjuna did was his work on the battlefield thinking only about the task at hand, and not about any consequences. So in a sense, there was a vow. All I did was to tell the Indraprastha contingent to blow their conches when I asked them to.'

Dhristadyumna grinned, 'But why was the vow redeemed on the death of Jayadratha?'

It seemed as if Arjuna did not have a voice of his own. Dhristadyumna spoke directly to Krishna who was now answering on his behalf.

'There was no one else around. He was an easy target. Everything just came together. The eclipse and Arjuna's arrow hitting Jayadratha. It just looked like too good a situation to not take advantage of. I thought on my feet. Admittedly, it's not one of the better stories floating around. But now, Arjuna's the man who can kill Kauravas at will. This belief will make a difference in the coming days.'

'If there are any more of them left after today!' cackled Drupada, enjoying his new-found status as a court jester. Some of us grinned politely. Dhristadyumna repeated the battle order for my benefit. I was to be in the left side of the square that was going to be led by Arjuna and Bhima. The right side would be managed by Dhristadyumna, Drupada and Shikhandi. The message was clear. There was a Pandava side of the battlefield, and a Panchala one. Satyaki and Chekitana were part of our side, and Virata was on the other. Clearly, he was leaving us to our devices, hoping to minimize damage to his troops that had lost many in their quest to hunt Drona.

Or maybe it was just my imagination. Maybe I was being too cynical. Like Arjuna and Bhima, maybe this was my way of dealing with grief. But Arjuna and Bhima knew of their loss. I did not know definitively about mine.

Hope, which I used to cling to in all my times of distress, was now clinging back to me, refusing to let go when I most wanted to lose it. If Prativindhya was dead and I knew for certain, at least I could mourn him and begin the painful process of banishing his memory from my thoughts.

The council meeting concluded and we went back to our tents to prepare for battle. Thoughts of Prativindhya distracted me and initially, I did not notice the absence of Vishakha. It was only when I saw an unfamiliar face holding my armour that I realized Vishakha was not there.

'Who are you? Where is Vishakha?' I growled. What could be so important for Vishakha to leave me on the morning of the battle?

'My lord, I am his helper,' said the man nervously. 'Man' is perhaps an exaggeration. He was a boy. 'He has gone to check the death lists. He asked me to keep your armour ready in case you came early.'

I nodded. For once, Vishakha was right to abandon me. I told the helper to prepare a leather armour and helmet and place it in my chariot. I'd grown tired of the metal breastplate. It was hot and my tired limbs could no longer support its weight. I walked to the chariot park still absorbed in my thoughts and my head had begun to throb by the time I reached. Vishakha was waiting for me.

'Still no word, my lord. He's still not on the death lists. He's bound to turn up somewhere. The battlefield is big and the camp is even bigger.'

The same old answers. Everyone wanted me to believe the boy was alive, yet I, in my heart of hearts, wanted to know he was dead. I was not only a bad soldier and brother, but a bad father as well. I ignored Vishakha, put on my helmet and stepped onto the chariot.

A light, leather armour was waiting for me. I put on a

muslin vest and strapped on the armour with Vishaka's help. I did not wear cuffs or any kind of armour on my arms. An extra round of throwing and stabbing spears were in my chariot having replaced the bows and arrows, regulation mace and battle axe that normally found place in a warrior's chariot.

I was ready by the time we reached the battlefield. I told Jivaka, who had escaped yesterday's carnage without me, to take me close to the front. I examined my chariot. Jivaka, lazy lout that he was, had not fixed my battle standard that had been cut from the top of the chariot umbrella. The chariot was still dusty from yesterday and lined with cuts and scrapes. It did not look like a prince's chariot. I was too tired to reprimand him, so I just stood on the chariot and let him take us to the battlefield.

The Kauravas were arranged in two pincers today. Our spies had thought they would be in the shape of a heron—a narrower version of the *garuda* formation we had set up yesterday. Their information had steadily become unreliable which was probably one of the reasons Dhristadyumna opted for a defensive formation today. There was too much information flying around. Best to play safe.

The wind was snapping at us today. While yesterday and most of the past fortnight, it had been still, today it appeared to be in a violent mood. I could see the Hastinapura and Anga banners being slapped awake by it at a distance. The wind was spitting in our ears and licking our faces. It started pushing us back, first in a friendly manner, and then with some strength. The dust rose from the ground as the wind scooped it up and sprayed it over us like we were its playthings.

The pincer closest to us was being manned by Karna, maybe

the Gandharas, and one of the Kauravas. I made my way to Arjuna's chariot in front and positioned my chariot next to his. I tried to not look at him for approval, but failed. Krishna caught my eye.

'Yudhishthira, I think Drona is on our side of the battlefield. I can see the Hastinapura and Anga banners up ahead. I think it would be wise for you to go to the other side. I have spoken to Virata about this.'

'I'm not afraid of Drona.'

'I know that, but without you, our cause is naught.'

I rolled my eyes. It seemed this line would be thrown at me till the end of my days. The string that dangled my puppet. He got off his charioteer's perch and walked over to my chariot, taking the step into its hollow.

'Arjuna and Bhima are not in very good shape right now. Without you, there will be no recognized leader of the Pandavas. Drupada and Virata are already beginning to get cold feet. If something happens to you, they won't trust your brothers with the throne. This entire effort will go to waste and they will have to parley or die on the field.'

He looked away for a moment, took a deep breath, and looked back at me. 'It's all well for Dhristadyumna to talk but we all know how important your presence is to this cause, especially in these circumstances. Please go to the other side. If Drona is still hunting you, it may be better to stay away from these parts. I'm dispatching a bodyguard with you.'

I nodded reluctantly. I had no wish to argue. Krishna was probably the only one left with some sanity. My own mind was drifting in and out of the quicksand of grief. I left sadly and it took me a little while to reach the other side. I avoided the Panchala troops as much as I could and made my way to Virata's Matsyas.

His chariot was among a line of chariots a few rows behind the front line and I displaced many of his troops to stand with him there. The front lines of the *sarvottabhadra* were occupied by men who held long pikes to ward off chariot and elephant attacks. Behind them, where I stood, were the chariots with archers, and behind us were regular foot soldiers and the few elephants we had left.

Virata looked at me and smiled. His face was pale and gaunt, and his grey hair cut close to his skull looked like a crown of ashes. He looked different today. He wore a green breastplate with a large lapis lazuli encrusted in the centre. In his left hand, he carried a matching helm, and the right one had a javelin. His eyes twinkled in his grey face, like fire in a graveyard.

'Good day to die, Yudhishthira,' he said, smiling and looking away.

The wind was loud, so our conches, drums, and horns blared even louder. Since yesterday's fight had gone on till the evening, we had feared today, it would start late. The battle actually started at the stipulated time. Our foot soldiers stood with their stabbing spears ready. We waited for the Kauravas to attack since the *sarvottabhadra* was a formation that reacted rather than acted.

The only problem was we couldn't see the enemy. The dust picked up and became a curtain around us, obstructing our vision. By the looks of it, a dust storm was coming. A chariot arose from the dust, then another, and finally an entire chariot troop came into vision. I couldn't make out the battle standards, but I knew the man with the grey beard and white armour at the head of their pincer well.

Drona.

Krishna had been wrong. Yet today, I felt no fear. I would kill him, or die in the attempt. The pincer careered sideways into our troops who were blinded by the dust storm and unable to respond to it in time. The dust wriggled through the crevices between armour and skin, and skipped merrily across our faces and into our eyes.

I covered my face with one hand as my other hand pawed the chariot cabinet for a piece of cloth. I found one. It was a long piece that I used to wipe weapons with once my sweat had been spent on them. I wrapped it across my face and kept a thin slit open for my eyes that were still on fire from the dust. The wind stopped for a moment; I rubbed my eyes clean and looked.

Virata's chariot was still next to mine but he was not in it. I looked around and saw him lying on the ground. An arrow through the palm of his hand and another through his throat. He lay on the ground, with his eyes wide open and his green armour coated with dust. It took a moment for me to realize that the blood that was rapidly covering the ground underneath him was actually his. I wanted to go and lift him, put him back in his chariot and have him admonish me for being weak one more time, when his own Matsyas came forward and removed his body behind a wall of shields.

All the men around me were fighting hard. The Kauravas were pushing at the front line with great force. Their chariots had been wary of our long spears but were still doing great damage from outside while our troops cowered under their shields.

I saw Drona shooting arrows into our midst without pause. He didn't take his usual half a moment to consider the target and decide where he should place the arrow. I picked up a javelin and flung it with all my might at him. The wind tossed it aside casually. I picked up another and waited for the wind to die down before I took aim.

Behind me, the Matsya line began to crumble. The spears in the front line wavered and Drona used his chariot as a battering ram to break through. Without their king or any visible leader, the men clattered into one another, trying to get out of Drona's way.

It could have turned into a rout but Drupada, with a large detachment of Panchala chariots, came from behind and allowed the Matsyas to escape between their rows. There was a brief pause in the proceedings. Drona and Drupada looked at each other from their chariots. Not a flicker of emotion on either face. They both lifted their bows and began mounting arrows.

The old fool. This was not a battle he would ever win in his seven births. I shouted at him to stop, but my voice was muffled by the cloth wrapped around my face and the dust-laden wind that whooped with glee in between us. The dust sprang into my eyes and I took a moment to rub them clean, hoping that when I opened them Drupada would still be alive.

It was Drona that I found reeling on his chariot, his back facing Drupada. Two arrows in his chest. Drupada had murder in his eyes and he plucked out two more arrows from his quiver, planting them between Drona's shoulder blades. Four arrows had now penetrated Drona. This was the closest any of the troops had gotten to hurting him. A few days ago, the old King Bhagadatta had given Drupada's ego a hammering. If Drupada could kill Drona now, Bharatvarsha would sing his praises for centuries.

I'd never hear the end of it.

He could run his mouth off all he wanted, the old goat. I saw him stretch his bowstring once more. Drona pulled out one of the arrows from his metal breastplate and sank to his knees as Drupada's arrow flew over him. He tried to pick out another arrow embedded in his armour, but an arrow from Drupada thudded into his arm, nearly toppling him. As he tried to stand up, another struck him square in the chest. He groaned loudly and fell back on his knees. Drupada took careful aim again. Drona seemed to be half-conscious.

A roar went up from the Panchala ranks and I don't think Drupada had ever been happier than he was in that moment. He loosened his grip on the string, took off the arrow, and raised his bow in victory. After this brief acknowledgement, he fixed the arrow back and took aim again, aware that such an opportunity to kill Drona would never come again. He released the arrow which flew straight at Drona's head.

Drona saw it coming, and twisted sideways, avoiding it. He wrenched out the arrow from his chest, grunting with pain, even as Drupada fumbled with an arrow on the string. Drona tottered up with the help of his bow and quickly picked out an arrow.

Where was this energy coming from?

Drupada's arrow flew and bounced off Drona's armour. Now Drona took aim and shot a single arrow. I couldn't see its flight. The next thing I saw was Drupada holding his neck up and falling on the chariot floor. I told Jivaka to rush towards his chariot and saw Drona take aim at me. He paused and the turban wrapped across my face along with the fact that I hadn't fixed my battle standard yet probably saved my life.

He flexed his bowstring, and then probably thinking I was not enough of a threat, loosened his grip. He sat down wearily on his chariot floor as it turned back into the safety of his lines. I made my way to Drupada who was surrounded by Panchalas. I took off the cloth wrapped around my face and walked through the crowd. The wind began to mewl again.

Drupada was lying down. A soldier had cradled his head on his lap. The arrow had gone through the side of his neck, taking much of it. The soldiers drew away when they saw me. His fingers beckoned weakly and I kneeled down. He wanted to say something, so I put my ear close to his mouth. He rasped something unintelligible. A pair of arms pushed me aside firmly. It was Dhristadyumna and behind him was Shikhandi. Both of them held their father's hands as he passed on to the next world.

I felt tears streaming down my face but wiped them quickly. The troops could not see me crying in the middle of battle. Dhristadyumna and Shikhandi looked distraught. I went over to Dhristadyumna and embraced him tightly. No words came out. Dhristadyumna pushed me aside and shouted for the troops to form up behind him. I saw Shikhandi—her face, like her brother's, had hardened.

A conch blast was heard. I looked ahead at the Kauravas, leading another charge towards us.

SUSHASANA

THE ARMY LOOKED like a crab. Two long claws which everyone called 'pincers' and a compact centre. Suyodhana and Guruji were leading one, and I was in the second one with Uncle Shakuni and Radheya. I told my troops to occupy the front rows and went and stood with uncle and Radheya two rows behind the front-line chariots.

Uncle didn't look happy to see me.

'Sushasana, you oaf, get behind!'

'There's no time, Uncle, look, war music's about to start.'

The banners of the Kuru began to flutter with those of Anga and Gandhara. The conches came out and everyone waited.

He called me an oaf, did he? What was his great achievement anyway? King of the Gandharas who were the best horsemen in Bharatvarsha, but a kingdom half the size of the Kurus. His sister had to marry our blind father to avoid being conquered by Grandsire Bhishma and he had fallen over himself slobbering around Grandsire to gain favour with the Kurus. He had made overtures towards Yudhishthira too who had rejected him outright. He had then wooed Suyodhana and they had orchestrated the game of dice for the kingdom. I still didn't know whether it was Suyodhana's great revenge, or Shakuni's. My mind travelled back to that fateful event.

We were in the hall of pleasure that evening. The Pandavas were our guests at Hastinapura. I was drunk. So drunk that I don't even remember what we were playing. All I remember was somewhere along the game we started betting. No harm in that. We would always bet horses or land or slaves. But then, Shakuni started goading Yudhishthira and made him bet his kingdom, and then his brothers. And the idiot bet it all.

I think we were taken more by the stupidity of it than anything. We started taunting the Pandavas and they became increasingly silent. Yudhishthira was so drunk he could barely see the numbers on the dice. Shakuni and Suyodhana were playing against him and beating him at every turn. It was such an emphatic victory that later, I heard that bards were making stories about the dice being loaded.

After the brothers were lost, Yudhishthira said he had nothing left to offer since everything was already ours. Shakuni smiled at him indulgently and reminded him that Draupadi wasn't. He then told him that he could win back everything on one dice throw if he bet Draupadi next.

The fool agreed.

I still didn't know why he did it. Maybe he didn't think the game was being played seriously, or that like cattle and land, wives could be sold off as wealth. Besides, I never understood how that relationship worked in the first place. Five men, one woman?

And why did they agree? I would never be comfortable sharing a wife with Suyodhana no matter how much I loved him. Sometimes I wondered how Draupadi felt about it. To divide her attention among five men, and then five sets of children, and to show them each the same level of trust and affection. It always seemed impossible to me. For that matter, Gandhari too. How did she feel when she was awoken one morning and told that she would have to marry a man who could not even see her beauty? They were both princesses of the biggest families in Bharatvarsha, and yet, they had no control on their own fate.

The chariots jerked into motion, bringing me back to the battlefield. The war music got louder. The stretch of land between the two armies diminished rapidly and we fell upon each other. I saw Radheya take out his arrows and release them gracefully. For a moment I wished I could use a bow like him but then realized that it wasn't worth the effort. To be honest, I felt using the bow as a weapon was a little pansy though I would never tell it to him. To kill someone from a distance was not very brave. I preferred the mace or the spear. Most people dismissed it as a club that relied only on the strength of the arms. Perhaps that was true, but to build the strength of the arms itself was an act of intelligence.

Shakuni moved in front of me, surrounded by his horsemen who swarmed about him. They went full tilt into the Pandava foot soldiers who were nearly swept away with the fury of the charge. Karna and Shakuni linked up and I saw them head towards Arjuna who was in the van.

Bhima was there too.

We never liked each other even as children. Both of us had similar aspirations of being the biggest bully in the playground. I had heard rumours that he had vowed to kill each and every one of us stepbrothers. I knew of at least four of us who had been killed by people other than him. Father had done the job with so many women that it had become difficult to keep count. All of us, noble bastards, lived in the palace and a few of us even knew each other's name, but there wasn't too much affection for anyone except Suyodhana—who everyone knew would be king.

Most of the stepbrothers, I suspected, were part of this war because they saw the merits of currying favour with Suyodhana, and not because of any real brotherly love. If, God forbid, the Pandavas won the war, they would probably have no hesitation in switching sides.

Bhima was surrounded by the Gandharas. I turned my attention to Radheya and Shakuni who had confronted Arjuna. There was no point getting involved in that fight. I didn't have half the skill Arjuna had. I looked around for some easy pickings. A Pandava chariot warrior a javelin's throw away had just finished a kill but had been wounded in the attempt. He stood in his chariot trying to tie a piece of cloth around his arm that had been cut. The wind had picked up. I could see the dust blowing on the other side of the field. The bowmen would be helpless in these conditions. All the better for me.

I told my charioteer to head in his direction. We gathered momentum. He saw me coming and lifted up a mace of his own, with less energy, wounded as he was. I swung my mace at his head as we passed and knocked his weapon out of his hand. The chariot screeched to a halt and I jumped out and ran towards him as he was picking up his mace. He was bent over and I kicked him hard in the chest. He fell and I brought my mace down on his skull. The sound of his head splitting was muffled by his helmet though the tiny river of blood surging across his face told me that I had hit him hard enough.

The dust was picking up and scattering around us. All of us began unravelling turbans and other pieces of cloth to cover our faces. A javelin flew over me. I turned around to see a chariot warrior readying another one. A prince for sure. Perhaps one of the Pandavas. I could not make out. He decided against throwing the javelin and took out a sword as his chariot advanced towards me. I fumbled as I tied the piece of muslin around my face and clenched my mace to meet him.

When he was close, he jumped off his chariot and advanced towards me. We circled each other as the dust billowed between us. He took a step forward and slashed. I stepped back to avoid it and tripped over some kind of weapon. I fell on my back and my mace clattered to my side. The warrior stood over me with his sword raised and removed the cloth from his face. It was Sahadeva.

He was about to bring the sword down on me when an arrow hit him in the side. He reeled and nearly fell over. I saw another arrow speed towards his head and spin off its path as the wind buffeted it. I looked at the source of the arrows. A chariot emerged through the dust and I saw Radheya upon it, nocking an arrow. He waited for the wind to stop and shot another arrow at Sahadeva. This time, the arrow hit a shield held by another warrior who wore armour identical to Sahadeva's and was also of the same build. His twin, Nakula. I looked around and found a sword on the ground. I picked it up and stood up.

Nakula and Sahadeva were standing together, holding swords. Radheya came up behind me on chariot and faced them. He would pick them off one by one. There was no way they could escape now. If they ran, I would finish them. Radheya drew an arrow and both the twins tensed. The next moment, a wave of dust blasted between us, momentarily blinding me.

When I cleared my eyes, the twins were gone.

RADHEYA

THE TWINS DIDN'T offer any fight. They just fled the scene. I saw them scamper away on their chariots. They were making a break for the other side of the battlefield. Shakuni's chariot pulled up next to me.

'They're fleeing,' he remarked, a little surprised.

'Unfortunately, yes. What news of the other side?'

Shakuni smiled wryly, 'Drona's broken through. Virata and Drupada have fallen from what I hear. But their long pikes are doing some damage. Suyodhana could use our help.'

I nodded. 'I'll leave Narasimha and some chariots here. We can go to the other side.'

He nodded back. I told my charioteer to head out and covered my face with some cloth. The day had begun well. Two senior Pandava generals were dead. If we added a little more heft to the pincer on that side, the war could tip in our favour. As it appeared, Arjuna and Bhima were being kept quiet on this side.

The dust was flying all around us, making combat difficult. The twins had gone back into the security of their lines. My chariot moved back into our lines and diagonally across the field to the other side. The dust was blowing with greater intensity and by the time I reached the other side, every one of the troops was unrecognizable—their faces covered with cloth or mail or whatever they could find. We pushed ahead to the front. The Pandavas had simply caved in. Whatever Drona had done, it had worked. If we won the war today, I would call him Guruji for the rest of his days.

I felt my lips curling into a smile. I had never really liked him before the last two days. Somehow, the *chakravyuha* had brought us closer. Abhimanyu's death was the glue that bound us.

I saw Suyodhana up front. He was directing his troops against Dhristadyumna's. He tried to say something, but his voice was muffled by the cloth he had tied across his face. He realized this, ripped off the cloth and shouted at me.

'What are you doing here?'

It was my turn to take off the cloth from my face. I took a deep breath, took it off and spoke quickly to avoid the dust from entering my mouth.

'Thought you would need some help.'

He tied the cloth again and began directing his troops. The wind had had enough, or so it seemed. In a little while, I would be able to use my bow again. Dhristadyumna's troops were getting pushed back. I readied my bow. The moment I had a chance, I would take his head off. Almost immediately, the wind calmed. I strung an arrow and pulled back the string, trying to get a shot of Dhristadyumna.

I could see him on foot, furiously hacking away with a sword as the men around him fell. He would suddenly get lost in a sea of humanity and then bob back up, looking more haggard every time. I tracked his movement and felt the wind pick up slightly. I decided to take the shot.

I shot the arrow directly at his forehead in a slightly downward motion. At the most, the wind would bend its arc towards his face or neck. A soldier came in the way of its path and I saw the arrow take him clean between the eyes. He slumped to the ground and I cursed.

The wind was picking up again. I had time for one more shot. I whipped out another arrow and pulled the string back to my ear. Before I could shoot, I saw three chariots rumble into view and forgot all about Dhristadyumna.

It was Bhima and the twins. I changed my aim and shot the arrow at Bhima, hoping desperately that the wind would stay low. It didn't, the arrow was picked up and flung aside.

Suyodhana's chariot came and took position next to me. To his left was Drona. His face looked worn and his armour had several punctures. He was leaning on his bow and wheezing. I had half a mind to tell him to go back and have the healers take care of him when I heard Bhima roar.

The three of them faced off against the three of us. Bhima lifted a spear and flung it with considerable strength at me. The wind could not deflect it from its trajectory and I jumped out of the chariot to avoid being impaled. It missed me by a hair's breadth and landed deep in the mud. I saw him readying another one. An arrow from Drona distracted him and he changed his focus.

I got back on the chariot and saw some chariots racing towards us and occupying the front line. The arrows began flying in our direction and I ducked to avoid the first wave. I peered over my chariot front and saw Bhima releasing the javelin in Drona's direction. The wind blew stronger this time and threw the javelin off course. Drona didn't retaliate as the heavy gusts of wind howling across the field were taking the arrows with them.

Suyodhana had gotten down on foot, and with a group of mace fighters, he was fighting his way through the Pandava front line. On his chariot, Bhima was charging towards us, holding his mace high. The wind stopped to take a breath.

I brought out an arrow and released it wildly in Bhima's direction hoping it would hit its mark. It flew wide as the wind began to pick up again.

Suddenly, I heard a conch over the din of the fighting. A white chariot with the Indraprastha battle standard and a dark charioteer headed slowly towards us into the front line.

It was Arjuna.

YUDHISHTHIRA

ARJUNA'S CHARIOT PULLED up next to me. My brother was still in his own world, very far from this one. Bhima with Nakula and Sahadeva had arrived and bolstered our line with some chariots. It had gotten desperate before that. Dhristadyumna had even gotten down and fought like a foot soldier to push back the Kaurava advance. I couldn't even throw my javelins because of the wind and had thought of getting down myself when Arjuna came.

Krishna spoke, 'We got word that this flank needed reinforcements so we came. I'd sent a messenger to bring Bhima and the twins. Satyaki's coming too.'

The wind stopped quite suddenly and I removed the cloth from my face. Krishna spoke to Arjuna and me.

'Let's go ahead. It'll do the troops good to see all five of you in the front line.'

I nodded a little reluctantly, but agreed. The Kauravas were steadily gaining ground on our side of the field. This could be the day we lost the war. Might as well lose it fighting. Sahadeva and Nakula joined to the left of me. Bhima, red-eyed and furious, came to Arjuna's right. The five of us stood together for the first time in the war.

Five Pandavas.

Arjuna took out his conch on Krishna's prompting and the rest of us followed his lead. We all blew together even as the troops ahead of us were getting slaughtered.

And then we charged.

Our troops cleared out and our chariots crashed straight into the Kaurava foot soldiers who desperately tried to get out of the way. I picked up a javelin and threw it towards a soldier and looked around for another. Nakula and Sahadeva were drawing arrows while Bhima had jumped off his chariot onto the ground and was swinging his mace wildly. Arjuna, three arrows in hand, was felling them faster than they could fill their lines. I stood in the middle of them—the eldest of this eccentric family whose only talent it seemed was to fight.

I picked up another javelin and threw it towards a chariot warrior who was approaching in the distance. Our own foot soldiers, emboldened by our charge, were screaming and following us. Even though our chariots had slowed down now, they were still advancing into the Kaurava line. A few chariot warriors tried to stem the tide but were felled immediately by Arjuna and the twins. It was turning into a rout. The Kauravas had beaten us to a pulp in this side of the battlefield, but we could still turn things around.

Then Drona came.

His chariot came alone, without any support. Maybe he thought he could kill us all. Before we could react, he had shot two arrows at Nakula and Sahadeva.

Both hit.

Nakula's breastplate got punctured, but not deeply.

Sahadeva's shoulder plate got scratched. A squadron of chariots were forming behind Drona. I braced myself to receive the next arrow but saw Drona duck under an arrow from Arjuna.

Krishna shouted at me, 'Surround him. Take the twins and Satyaki.'

Where was he going with this? Drona had been hunting me for the past four days and I had only escaped by the breadth of a grain of the dust that had been frolicking about us just a few moments ago.

He must have seen my confusion. He mouthed a word slowly, looking into my eyes.

'Abhimanyu.'

I nodded and signalled to the twins and Satyaki who had pulled in right next to me.

'Going to get the old man, are we?' he said, grinning.

I nodded. For all his foolishness, he was here when we needed him the most. Drona was almost isolated from his troops who still hadn't reformed. This was our only chance. Our chariots moved in a wide arc around him as Arjuna kept him occupied. From the other end, Bhima and Dhristadyumna—now on a chariot—swung around him along with a few chariots. The resistance on the way was scant and we circled around him in no time. He was trapped in our *chakravyuha* now.

But he didn't seem to notice. Satyaki and a few chariots formed a ring around us and fought off the Kauravas who had begun to realize that their commander-in-chief was surrounded by the enemies. I saw Suyodhana running like a madman only to be grazed by an arrow from Satyaki. He swivelled and found refuge behind a chariot.

Radheya's chariot came into the fray and I saw him

desperately trying to get the retreating troops to turn around and fight. I turned my attention to Drona. This would have to be done quickly. We would never get an opportunity like this again. Satyaki's chariots blocked his advance and we closed in on Drona. He was surrounded by us.

He did not flinch. If anything, the arrows came more relentlessly than before, with greater speed and urgency. Twice, Arjuna ducked from his shafts and Bhima actually had to cower down in his chariot to avoid getting hit.

And I? I stood behind him, with a clear sight of his back. My hand clenched a javelin; I was frozen with fear. I could throw the javelin and Drona would be dead. We were barely a few feet away from each other. Even I could make this throw. I wondered briefly what his face was like at that moment. Did he look tired or angry? Were the lines sunken in his face like a river in a drought or did the flesh ooze over it? I hadn't seen his face, it seemed, since forever. I saw only his mask of anger on the battlefield. The face that he had never shown us when he was our Guruji.

I saw Bhima's chariot sidle next to Arjuna. Bhima hunched over his chariot and spoke to Krishna, even as Arjuna kept Drona occupied. He listened intently to what Krishna had to say, and then, moved his chariot ahead. His voice rose above the clamour of the battlefield.

'Your son is dead, Drona. Ashwatthama is dead.'

Drona stopped for a moment. Arjuna had an arrow fixed but did not take the shot.

'He died a little while back. I killed him myself. Beat his brains all over the field.'

Drona's hands fell to the side. Arjuna still did not take

the shot. I wanted to scream at him but my own tongue was frozen. Drona stood in the centre of us. He didn't lift his bow and we kept our weapons on our sides.

'His body is somewhere in the back. I'll send what's left back to you once the jackals have had their fill,' said Bhima cruelly.

Drona's back hunched. Guruji, with a posture that would have put an iron pillar to shame, looked small. He turned around and saw me. I looked into his eyes and saw the sadness in them questioning me. I heard his voice, hoarse and quavering.

'Is…is it true?'

Of all the people in the battlefield, he had to ask me? What would I tell him? I had no idea whether Ashwatthama was dead or not.

I looked into his eyes and remembered what Krishna told me a while ago.

'Abhimanyu.'

'He's dead. Bhima killed him,' I replied, without any emotion in my voice. My chariot jolted a little and sunk into the ground that was wet with blood now. Our gaze held for a few moments as he looked into my eyes to find even a trace of a lie. After a few moments, he lifted his bow and half-heartedly shot an arrow at Arjuna that went over him. Arjuna did not retaliate. None of us did, not even Bhima.

We stood around him awkwardly in our chariots. He looked around and I noticed his eyes had become wild. He wiped the tears that paved the dust on his face and looked, for the first time since I had known him, like an old man. He looked into my eyes again, pleading for me to tell him Ashwatthama was alive. I held his gaze and refused to let go.

The sound behind me was growing louder. I looked behind

to see Radheya and Suyodhana fighting their way through Satyaki's men. Someone had to do something—but we were all helpless.

I saw Drona look at all of us. He was weeping uncontrollably now. He put his bow down and sat down on his chariot. His charioteer peered at him, not knowing what to do. I saw him whisper something to Drona, but he just put his head in his hands and sobbed.

We stood in our chariots looking at each other like idiots as the commander-in-chief of our enemy's army sat in his chariot and wept. I saw Dhristadyumna approach him purposefully. He had a sword in his hand. A part of me wanted to tell him to stop, another part wanted to look away and let him do what he had to. I had felt this way when Grandsire had fallen, and far too many times over the course of the war. I did what I did every time. Nothing.

Dhristadyumna walked from behind Drona and pushed his charioteer away. He raised the sword and struck him hard on the head. Drona fell and Dhristadyumna kept hacking at him. A few moments later, he picked up Drona's head and bayed loudly, raising it for the army to see.

Panic is faster than thought.

The amount of time it takes to think or even comprehend a problem is much less than it takes for one's survival instinct to act. The Kaurava troops howled and began to disintegrate when they saw Dhristadyumna brandishing Drona's head.

The only person who stood his ground was Radheya.

RADHEYA

Drona's eyes were looking at me. Maybe it was a fault in my vision. I blinked to correct it. They were still looking at me. My vision blurred a little. Was 'he' really looking at me? Or 'it'? Was it still human or did disembodied heads have no identity? I shook my head vigorously. I felt afraid for the first time in days. My chest squeezed tightly and I instinctively looked around for Drona.

And then the panic began.

There are two ways to respond to panic. You either run or freeze in your spot. I froze and watched mutely as the men around me ran. I looked around and saw Shakuni staring at Drona's head, his mouth open. His charioteer, sensing danger, turned his chariot around, and his cavalry began to retreat.

An arrow flew past me. And then, another one. I saw a third arrow headed straight towards me, and I knew that if it kept its path, it would hit me in the centre of my forehead. My feet were stuck to the chariot floor. The arrow flew closer and I was powerless to do anything but wait for it to strike me. The wind rose and moved the arrow a little to the side. It whizzed past me and I felt the edge of the arrow breach the flesh of my neck with a sharp pinch.

The arrow's touch shook me from my cage of fear. I picked up my conch and blew desperately, hoping it would stop the troops or at least get their attention. I blew and blew, and expended my throat into the conch but the troops passed me without bothering to even look at me. If they looked at anything, it was Drona's head with his eyes still staring out into the world—held by Dhristadyumna's hand.

I looked around me. Suyodhana's chariot was driving towards me and a little ahead of him was Ashwatthama. I told my charioteer to intercept Ashwatthama. I did not want him to see his father in this state.

My chariot skidded in front of his, even as his charioteer reared the horses to avoid crashing into my chariot. I flailed my arms desperately hoping to hold his gaze before it drifted towards his father's head.

I don't think he recognized his father at first. He looked at the head being dangled about like a puppet in Dhristadyumna's hand. He had removed Drona's helmet and held the head by its hair. The face was streaked with blood owing to Dhristadyumna's relentless pawing. Shouting 'Drona! Drona!', Dhristadyumna hoisted the head high for everyone to see like it was some kind of ghoulish prize.

It was then that Ashwatthama saw his father. I saw his expression change from curiosity to surprise to horror within a moment. His mouth opened, but no words came out. His bow clattered to the chariot floor.

What was he thinking? I got off my chariot and saw Suyodhana who ran to Ashwatthama before I reached him. We held Ashwatthama and turned his head away. Suyodhana buried his head into his armour. I picked up Ashwatthama's bow and fought off some Pandava soldiers who were chasing our retreating forces.

A few of Suyodhana's Leopard Guards surrounded our chariots and we began to retreat. The Pandava front line was nearly upon us and I dispatched arrow after arrow into the mass of soldiers.

Dhristadyumna, with Drona's head, came closer to us. He carried no weapon but shouted to his troops to drive them forward. I felt a hand hold the bow and turned to see Ashwatthama. His eyes were dry and he said nothing. He pulled the bow out of my mine and picked up an arrow to begin shooting. This needed a more drastic intervention.

Suyodhana left Ashwatthama's chariot and ran back to his own. I returned to mine and saw Ashwatthama's chariot heading full tilt into the Pandava horde towards Dhristadyumna. He was as good as dead. They would pull him off his chariot and hack him to pieces. Suyodhana's chariot followed Ashwatthama closely. I cursed and told my charioteer to head towards them.

Soon it was just the three of us protected by a thin line of Leopard Guards, surrounded by an ocean of Pandava troops. They were being bullied forward by Dhristadyumna who was brandishing Drona's head and roaring at us. Suyodhana could not use a bow so Ashwatthama and I took over the killing. Ashwatthama was spectacular. He caught Satyaki on the shoulder with a crescent-headed arrow and Satyaki fell off his chariot. Another arrow caught Bhima in the gut of his armour, and Bhima crashed to his knees. Three arrows caught three chariot warriors in their faces and one went through the neck of one warrior, into the face of another.

He wanted to get as close to Dhristadyumna as possible. Suyodhana got down on foot, removed his helmet and took up a position at the head of the Leopard Guard. He wielded his mace, brutally beating away the oncoming men. I was pouring in all my arrows into the mass of Pandava troops that kept getting closer to us.

The Leopard Guards were finally overwhelmed. I saw Suyodhana plunge into a mass of Pandava swordsmen. My chariot was surrounded by Pandava soldiers. I shot one at point-blank range, and another one who was trying to assail my charioteer. I put another arrow onto my string when I felt a pair of hands drag me from the back. I fell down and someone tore my helmet off. From my position on the ground, I saw three Pandava soldiers hover over me. Astonishingly, the only thought that ran through my head had nothing to do with survival—these bastards would never drag a royal out of his chariot. They did this to me only because I was a *suta*.

One put his foot on my chest, pinning me down, and another raised a sword. I kept my eyes open. I would not show fear in the face of death.

I didn't need to.

The soldier fell to his knees and slumped on top of me. The pressure of the foot on my body was taken off. Someone hauled the body of my would-be killer off me. I blinked. A hand was thrust in my direction, and I was pulled up.

It was a Narayani. He nodded at me and went forward. I looked around and saw Kritavarma leading a charge into the Pandava troops with Narayani chariots arranged perfectly in a wedge. They broke through and scattered the Pandavas. I got on my chariot and headed towards Drona's head that was still held by Dhristadyumna. Ashwatthama was fighting his way there himself, surrounded by Narayanis now. Drona's head had now become more important than the outcome of the war. We could not let the head of our commander-in-chief remain in the hands of the enemy.

I saw Ashwatthama take out an arrow and take careful aim. It flew straight and hit Dhristadyumna hard on his helmet. He fell over and the head fell into the mud. A group of Narayanis swarmed forth through the Pandava lines and after a short and brutal scramble, picked up the head and returned to our force.

I joined Ashwatthama, along with the Narayanis, and we began driving the Pandavas back. Arjuna, Nakula and Sahadeva appeared and organized their lines to deal with our onslaught. The wind began blowing again. This time, with greater intensity. It pulled up sheets of dust and spread it over us. We covered our faces but the dust slithered in and writhed against our faces. The wind sprayed dust into our eyes and blinded us once again.

The wind, it seemed, was putting on a performance. It whistled loudly and the dust pirouetted in front of us. We stood on our chariots—mute and unwilling spectators, waiting for it to finish. The wind seemed to sense our impatience and the dust moved with greater intensity causing many of us to cough in applause.

Both armies stopped fighting. Nature, it seemed, wanted peace. Yesterday, her device for intervention had been the sun, today, it was the wind. This was a dust storm. All we could do was sit and try not to be blown away. We would not win if we fought the wind. It howled around us and some of the soldiers began to sit down. I spotted Suyodhana's chariot and took my chariot to him slowly as the wind threatened to tip the chariot over.

I removed the cloth I had tied on my face. 'We can't fight like this,' I said, only to have dust cram itself in my mouth.

Kritavarma was next to him.

'I agree. Let's retreat. Call an end to the day. Pandavas won't mind, they've suffered major losses. It'll do our men good too.'

'It's barely noon,' said Suyodhana.

'The wind's not going anywhere,' replied Kritavarma curtly.

Suyodhana nodded.

'Ask Drona to parley with the Pandavas.'

There was a brief awkward silence.

'Guruji is no longer with us,' said Kritavarma gently.

Suyodhana pursed his lips and looked confused. For the first time in the battle, there was no elder giving him counsel.

'Make the troops retreat in order, guarding their backs and flanks. The Pandavas will get the idea. They won't be stupid enough to attack us in the middle of a dust storm anyway. Relay the word across the line. Tell the war chroniclers to announce the day's end once we've retreated,' I said.

Kritavarma nodded and barked for some messengers. The troops began withdrawing. Most of them in our part of the field were his Narayanis anyway, so they withdrew in perfect formation. Some of the Narayanis and I withdrew last to avoid unnecessary bloodshed. There was little resistance from the Pandavas.

Both the armies had met their match.

THE FIFTEENTH NIGHT

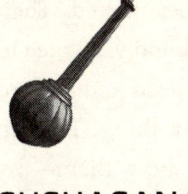

SUSHASANA

IT WAS EARLY evening and the dust was still flying when I reached the council tent. I was late but the tent was silent when I entered. In the centre of the tent, Suyodhana stood with Shakuni, looking lost. The Speaking Staff was in his hand but he wasn't speaking.

With Guruji gone, he was the only one who could lead us. And yet, he didn't look anything like a leader. He looked like a boy lost in a mela, without any idea of how to get home. I didn't know what to say. I wanted to do something, but I was no leader. I could not give commands. I was good at taking them. And I would never let Suyodhana down if he told me to do anything.

My mind went back to that day in Hastinapura, when we had beaten the Pandavas at dice. The mood that day had intoxicated me as it had all of us. So when Suyodhana asked Yudhishthira if he was man enough to bet Draupadi, and he agreed, I almost knew he was going to lose. And he did.

Maybe I got carried away, but a chance to rub the Pandava noses into the ground was too good to pass up. If I ever had a chance to do it again, I probably would. I remember the Pandavas sitting around the little dice board, looking bewildered. Their bodies were stiff with anger. If they weren't so blindly devoted to Yudhishthira, one of them would have gone ahead and slapped him. I know I would have. A woman is not a thing. To even agree to bet her was wrong. And I would show them—my morally superior half-cousins—the error of their ways. Always on the right side of Grandsire Bhishma and Guruji, where were they now?

I remember laughing then. The scene was vivid in my mind. I said, 'I need to inspect the property. Let's get it here!' I told some of our brothers to bring her into the room. They obeyed me, and a few moments later, she followed. Still, there was no word from the Pandavas. By now, all my half-brothers had begun celebrating our 'conquest' of the kingdom and were goading them. Bhima in particular looked like he would kill us all.

She came into the hall. She looked beautiful—'resplendent', I believe is a word in favour with the bards these days—and her eyes rolled when she saw Yudhishthira and the brothers hunched over the dice board.

'What have you gone and done now, husband?'

'He's bet you off. You're ours,' I slurred.

'The queen of Indraprastha is not a thing. And certainly not your possession,' she said, her eyes narrowing at me from the bridge of that magnificent nose. Such rage. No wonder she kept all the boys in check.

'It is now. Your man has gone ahead and bet you off in a game. You belong to us now. The sooner you start behaving like it, the better.'

My voice rose and I saw other people had entered the tent including the elders and Krishna who came and stood next to her, while her husbands kept to themselves.

'A game played by drunks has no meaning; surely you should know that by now. You look like you've played and lost enough. You certainly don't have the grace of a winner.'

Her haughtiness annoyed me, but also aroused me a little. I walked over to her and looked her in the eye.

'You're ours. And I can do with you as I please.'

She continued looking into my eyes without any fear, as if daring me. Was this what my manhood was reduced to? A woman could look me in the eye without trembling? If she got away with it, all my servants would. I would never hear the end of it.

I put my hand on her shoulder and pulled at her sari. In that moment, Krishna struck my hand and came in between us. Bhima finally cracked. He bellowed and rushed at me. All my brothers came in between and it took all the palace guards to separate us.

What happened next is common knowledge. The Kuru elders banished the Pandavas for thirteen years since they had been foolish enough to bet their kingdom and were undeserving of it. I suspect they did it more to keep Bhima from murdering us. In any case, no one was happy with what I did and the bards even had the gall to say the war was revenge for the incident with Draupadi. If that was the case, what stopped them from killing me anytime over the past thirteen years for her satisfaction, even if it meant sacrificing the kingdom completely? The Pandavas wanted a kingdom, and so did we. It was as simple as that. At least we never hid it or tried to appear superior about it.

They say I shouldn't have done what I did—that laying hands on Draupadi was wrong. For the first time in thirteen years

I began to feel like maybe I shouldn't have. The bards made up all kinds of stories. They said that when I tried to remove Draupadi's saree, the cloth stretched endlessly as I pulled it, and miraculously prevented me from taking it off her body. Some of the stories even said that this was divine protection—from Krishna, of all people. Over the years, I began to hear new stories. One even said that Bhima was going to drink my blood and eat my innards as revenge for laying hands on her. Maybe if I had never laid hands on Draupadi and let the Pandavas leave quietly with their pride and kingdom in place, we would never have had to fight this war? Shakuni's voice interrupted my thoughts.

'We've lost Dronacharya today. But we haven't lost the war. As the oldest person in this council, I have taken it upon myself to provide guidance to you all.'

He paused, stared at the ground, and then looked back at us.

'In a war, there can only be loss. This much I know. And I'm sure all of you do as well by now. But now is not the time to dwell on our losses. Not when we have two *akshauhinis* of troops to the single odd *akshauhini* of the Pandavas. We lost our commander-in-chief today, but the Pandavas lost more troops. That is the simple fact. They also lost Drupada and Virata, their two most senior councilmen.

'Why am I telling you all this? To arouse hope—to drag it out of the quicksand of sadness we find ourselves in? No, I'm not so vain as to think that my words will do that. Instead, I am suggesting that the Pandavas are in worse shape than we are. The war is almost at an end and we need to finish it on *our* terms. Dronacharya was a fine battle commander and a great servant of the Kurus. All our condolences are with you,

Ashwatthama,' he said, looking at Ashwatthama briefly.

I stood on my toes and saw him. He stood in a corner. He nodded and then looked down, perhaps embarrassed by the attention. I heard how he had charged single-handedly and retrieved his father's head. Later, once the troops had disengaged and the Pandavas had left the field, he had gone with a search party and located his body. There must have been over a thousand on the field and he had gone through each and every one of them to find his father.

'We need a commander now who can match your father's energy, or at least come close to it.'

Shakuni looked at Suyodhana.

'There are many excellent generals among us. And while we will put the issue to vote, in my opinion there is only one person who can lead our cause.'

YUDHISHTHIRA

THE TENT SEEMED empty tonight without old Virata and Drupada. Both Dhristadyumna and Shikhandi were silent. They would wait till dawn to cremate their father. They looked tired and not in any frame of mind to discuss tomorrow's formation. Not that there were too many formations we could execute with what was left of our troops.

A light haze of dust hung inside the council room. It was early evening, and even the sun, hidden as it was by the dust, had given up for the day and had retreated into the clouds. The Kauravas had disengaged and left the field first. The dust had made fighting impossible. We had left soon after them.

In truth, the early end to hostilities was good for us. We had lost far too many men today, and two of our senior-most commanders. Drona's death also weighed on my mind. A part of me felt I should have been glad that he was gone, no longer tormenting our forces, or threatening me with capture. That one of the murderers of Abhimanyu was dead.

The other part of me felt deep sadness at the loss of my Guru. Did any of my brothers feel this? Arjuna sat on his chair quietly while Krishna sat next to him, his eyes closed in thought.

Nakula and Sahadeva were bruised and were almost asleep, but would be able to fight tomorrow. Bhima slouched back on his chair. Even Satyaki was not his cheerful self. Chekitana had been cut by a sword in the latter half of the day, and sat silently in the corner. He must be secretly thrilled, the boy. His first real war wound. He could count himself among the veterans now. Without Drupada or Virata, it fell on me, as the eldest, to commence the meeting.

'Dhristadyumna, Shikhandi, we're all deeply sorry for your loss. Your father was like a parent to the five of us as well. We would never have been able to fight the war without him or Virata.'

For a moment, I feared it had come out too quickly and insincerely. I had practised the speech before I came inside, knowing fully well that when providing condolences, the way the words were delivered was as important as the words themselves. Drupada had been my ally, and my father-in-law. There had to be a sense of formality to my condolence. At the same time, there had be genuine grief at the loss of a family member. Dhristadyumna and Shikhandi had to feel that they were not grieving alone. Both of them nodded. I was silent. I had said my piece and did not know where to divert the conversation.

Bhima did it for me.

'Well, Drona is finally dead. I'm glad that Dhristadyumna put things right. If we had done it so many years ago in the sabha, maybe this day would never have come. The loss of your father was terrible, but he would be proud of you both.'

'He was your Guru, Bhima. You address him by his name?' Satyaki spoke in an emotionless voice.

'Drona stopped being my Guru when he decided to take arms against me and my brothers.'

'Do all of you feel this way?'

Now awake, Nakula and Sahadeva did not say anything. But Nakula nodded in agreement. Arjuna looked at the ground and did not speak.

'Yudhishthira, you lied to him about his son,' said Satyaki looking at me now.

'Yes, I did. So what?'

I was tired of being judged. For the sabha, for the war, for my inability to fight and now, for killing an adversary. It seemed nothing I would ever do would escape scorn. It was bad enough that the people would talk about it, but my own allies?

'We need to hold ourselves to a higher standard. Just because they fight like savages doesn't mean we have to as well.'

'What do you mean?' I said, hurt and genuinely curious to understand what Satyaki was thinking.

'When the war is over, people won't remember that we won, but how we won. Killing Drona by sneaking up behind him is hardly the work of a warrior or the future king of the Panchalas,' he said, again, in an emotionless drawl.

'And Bhurisravas? Do you forget him so easily?' I said, trying to match the calmness of his tone.

'There was already a duel between Bhurisravas and me. There was none between Drona and Dhristadyumna.'

Dhristadyumna stood up. Bhima leaped out of his seat to stop him from ripping out Satyaki's tongue. Satyaki was not perturbed.

'Killing a defenseless old man is as bad as killing a young one. I say this not to upset you, Dhristadyumna. Your father was truly the best of us. But I say this as a well-wisher to both your clans. We cannot stoop to their levels.'

'Whose side are you on, you filth?!' shouted Dhristadyumna. Shikhandi got up and took out a dagger she had concealed in her belt. Suddenly, the whole council was out of control. Nakula, Sahadeva and Chekitana stood up to block her from Satyaki.

I bellowed, 'Stop! Stop!'

I saw Krishna take Satyaki aside, out of the tent. And it was with great difficulty that we managed to get Dhristadyumna and Shikhandi to sit down and listen to us.

'Tell him to leave. Now. Otherwise we will,' Dhristadyumna said curtly; his voice was trembling.

'He was completely out of line, Dhristadyumna. I apologize on his behalf.'

Krishna stepped in with the wind howling behind him.

'I spoke to Satyaki. It's been a long day. He was tired. He apologizes for his comments. They were insensitive at a time like this. He will come in person and apologize in the morning.' He paused for a moment. 'As I said, he was tired and the strain has begun to show.'

Dhristadyumna nodded and didn't pursue the subject. He probably knew, just as his father did, that we needed every man possible to win. Now more so than ever. I felt a tightness in my chest. I would now have to perform the role of Drupada and Virata for the council. I would have to pacify everyone and keep us together. I felt the weight of our cause on me more than ever.

Bhima diverted the conversation again.

'You were right about Drona, Krishna. How did you know he would get so affected by Ashwatthama?'

'I didn't. It just seemed worth a try.'

'Well, you weren't too far from the truth, I'll tell you that. The evening before, I killed an elephant called Ashwatthama. Remember I was telling you, Yudhishthira?'

I didn't, but nodded anyway. There was something strange about the way Krishna was going about this. We called an end to the council soon. No one was in the mood to talk further.

Outside the tent, I confronted Krishna.

'Krishna, a word.'

He turned around and looked at me.

'You told Bhima to taunt Drona?'

'Yes,' he said, a little surprised.

'Knowing fully well that Drona may have killed him for killing Ashwatthama?'

He was silent.

'Yesterday, you took Arjuna right into the depths of their army?'

'I was with him myself. If something happened to him, I would have died as well.'

'I heard you ordered Ghatotkacha to attack Radheya. Shikhandi told me. She said the boy died fighting bravely.'

Krishna was silent for a moment. 'What are you getting at, Yudhishthira?'

'You've been responsible for keeping me in the back. As bait for Drona. I've nearly been killed twice.'

'This is war, Yudhishthira. Men get killed. You're getting paranoid.'

Was I? Or was there something in the fact that Krishna was deliberately putting us in harm's way. He and Arjuna had been away the day of the *chakravyuha*. Was that part of his ploy?

I blinked and looked at him.

'We're all puppets to you, aren't we? To be moved when you please,' I mumbled bitterly.

Krishna looked at me sadly.

'You're tired. I will not say any more. Only this. There was a letter from Uttaraa in the morning. She is with child. They think it will be a boy. Abhimanyu lives on.'

The news gave me scant joy. I turned around in a daze and walked back without acknowledging him. My mind was whirring with possibilities. Was Krishna trying to put a Yadava on the Kuru throne? Was he systematically planning our destruction? Or was he trying to protect us as he claimed?

What was I thinking? Was the war playing tricks on my mind? Vishakha was standing outside my tent. He looked visibly upset, as if he had been crying.

'What's the matter, Vishakha?' I asked, without genuinely caring.

He sobbed.

'Your son, sire. Prativindhya...'

ARJUNA

YOU'RE STILL HERE, aren't you?

Listening to your old man ramble on about life, war, 'duty' and all the things he never had time to talk about when you were growing up. Bear with me a little longer, son.

You've been with me for two days now, guiding me across the battlefield. I've felt the strength of your arms draw the bowstring to my ears when I no longer had the desire to fight. I've felt the keenness of your vision look out into the battlefield when I was too tired to keep my eyes open. I've felt your heart pump blood into my legs and command them to move, when all I wanted was to hold myself still in the face of the first arrow that would have me.

I won't keep you further.

We spend our entire lives preparing ourselves to deal with loss. We use every trick in our means—whether it involves convincing ourselves that nothing will happen to the ones we love while we are around, or creating a wall between ourselves and the people around us, so that they can never know that we really love them.

But there is nothing that can help a man prepare for loss.

No shield, no magic charm, no trick of the mind that can fill the void when someone you loves is taken away or decides to leave. The best you can do—the only thing you can do—is face the void, plunge through it, and hopefully survive it.

I know you don't want to leave until you're sure I can take your loss. If I could, I would ask you to stay with me for the rest of my mortal life. I would ask you to hold my hand and walk me through the void as you did through the battlefield. And I know you would. But this is a journey I can only complete without you.

You yourself have a journey to make now. And I've kept you from it for two days. You will go to a better place, of this I am certain. You won't be travelling alone. There is a part of me that is forever in you. As there is something of you that will never leave me.

Goodbye, Abhimanyu. I will meet you in the next life.

EPILOGUE

He preferred being called Devadutta these days. He had always hated the name 'Bhishma'. Such a violent name for a man who had never really cared for it. Bhishma was not a name as much as an identity—a mask that needed to be worn. Now, there was no need for a mask. And there was no one to wear the mask for.

He still kept getting messages from the field. Sanjaya Gavalgani performed the courtesy. Devadutta couldn't change anything anymore. Neither could Bhishma for that matter. But as a Kuru he needed to know how the next generation would shape the kingdom. If there would be a next generation at all.

Drona had fallen that day. He had felt sad initially. He would have liked to say goodbye. The end was coming near for him too. But he told himself that one could never really say goodbye. There would always be a part of Drona with him. A memory, a ghost he would visit till the end of his days.

He heard feet shuffling outside the tent. The number of visitors had diminished day by day. He didn't mind it. The company of his thoughts were enough for him these days. Most visitors came to tell him that someone was dead or simply came to seek his blessings.

He had become a dispenser of blessings these days. That was his only role. It gave him some happiness. This is how the elderly should be. They should transmit their energy to the young. Give them good thoughts. He spent most of his time raising his hand with his palm facing the beneficiary of the blessing.

Devadutta wondered who was seeking blessings this late.

'Grandsire?'

'Come in, Radheya,' he said, recognizing the voice. The pain in his body had subsided but had left him extremely weak. His mind was alert however, and though his voice hobbled through his throat slowly, it still managed to escape.

'Drona fell.'

'Dronacharya.'

'He was no Acharya of mine,' the reply came pat.

'What brings you here?' he sighed.

There was a pause.

'Something happened today. I...I wanted to tell someone about it.'

'Go on then.'

'We were gathered in the council tent after the day's battle. Shakuni as the senior-most general suggested we vote for the next commander-in-chief. The allies voted unanimously.'

He paused again. He appeared uncomfortable.

'I lead the Kurus now. I will protect Suyodhana. I promise.'

Devadutta was silent. He slowly extended his arm. Radheya clasped it and began to sob.

Devadutta spoke gently, *Vijayibhava putra*. Victory be with you.'

GLOSSARY

Akshauhini:	An army corps comprising chariots, elephants, infantry and cavalry
Akhara:	Training ground
Ankini:	An army brigade
Atirathi:	An elite warrior
Chakravyuha:	A circular battle formation that was responsible for many Pandava casualties on the thirteenth day of the war
Gandiva:	The name of Arjuna's bow
Garuda:	A battle formation arrayed in the shape of the celestial eagle
Maharathi:	An elite warrior, superior to an *atirathi*
Rishabh:	a musical note
Sakata:	A box-shaped battle formation
Sarvottabhadra:	A compact square-shaped battle formation
Shakti:	The name of Radheya's iron-headed arrows
Suta:	In this book and *The Thirteenth Day*, it refers to charioteers and is used as a derogatory term
Vatsadanta:	An arrow with a head shaped like a calf's tooth
Vijaya:	The name of Radheya's bow
Vijayibhava putra:	'Be victorious, son'
Yavana:	Foreigner